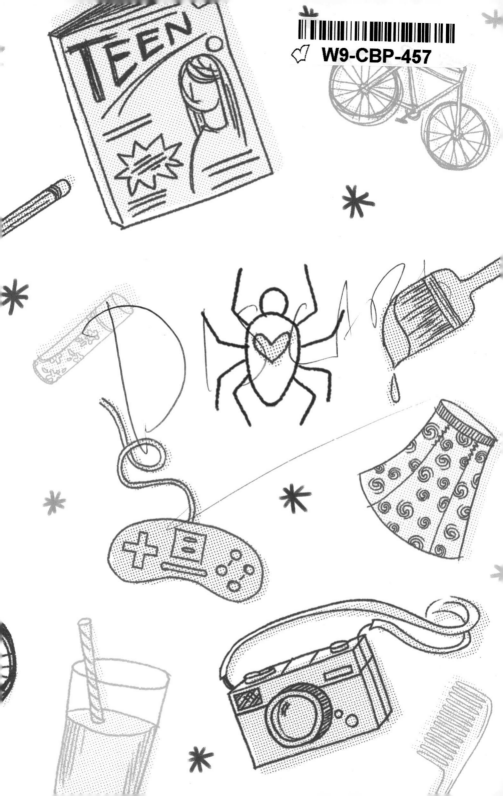

GEORGE

GEORGE

ALEX GINO

Scholastic Press / New York

Library of Congress Control Number: 2014957885

ISBN 978-0-545-81254-2

10 9 8 7 6 5 4 3   16 17 18 19

Printed in the U.S.A.   23
First edition, September 2015

Book design by Ellen Duda

TO YOU,
FOR WHEN YOU FELT
DIFFERENT

TABLE OF CONTENTS

chapter I

SECRETS

George pulled a silver house key out of the smallest pocket of a large red backpack. Mom had sewn the key in so that it wouldn't get lost, but the yarn wasn't quite long enough to reach the keyhole if the bag rested on the ground. Instead, George had to steady herself awkwardly on one foot while the backpack rested on her other knee. She wiggled the key until it clicked into place.

Stumbling inside, she called out, "Hello?" No lights were on. Still, George needed to be certain the house was empty. The door of Mom's room was open and the bedsheets were flat. Scott's room was unoccupied as well. Sure that she was alone, George went into the third bedroom, opened the closet door, and surveyed the pile of stuffed animals and assorted toys inside. They were undisturbed.

Mom complained that George hadn't played with any of the toys in years, and said that they should be donated to needy families. But George knew they were needed here, to guard her most prized and secret collection. Fishing beneath the teddy bears and fluffy bunnies, George felt for a flat denim bag. Once she had it in hand, she ran to the bathroom, shut the door, and turned the lock. Clutching the bag in tightly wrapped arms, George slid to the ground.

As she tipped the denim bag on its side, the silky, slippery pages of a dozen magazines fell out onto the tiled bathroom floor. Covers promised HOW TO HAVE PERFECT SKIN, TWELVE FRESH SUMMER HAIRCUTS, HOW TO TELL A HOTTIE YOU LIKE HIM, and WILD WINTER WARDROBES. George was only a few years younger than the girls smiling at her from the glossy pages. She thought of them as her friends.

George picked up an issue from last April that she had looked through countless times before. She browsed the busy pages with a crisp *flip-flip-flip* that stirred up the faint smell of paper.

She paused on a photo of four girls at the beach. They modeled swimsuits in a line, each striking a pose. A guide on the right-hand side of the page recommended various styles based on body type. The bodies looked the same to George. They were all girls' bodies.

On the next page, two girls sat laughing on a blanket, their arms around each other's shoulders. One wore a striped bikini; the other wore a polka-dot one-piece with cutouts at the hips.

If George were there, she would fit right in, giggling and linking her arms in theirs. She would wear a bright-pink bikini, and she would have long hair that her new friends would love to braid. They would ask her name, and she would tell them, *My name is Melissa*. Melissa was the name she called herself in the mirror when no one was watching and she could brush her flat reddish-brown hair to the front of her head, as if she had bangs.

George flipped past flashy ads for book-bag organizers, nail polish, the latest phones, and even tampons. She skipped over an article on how to make your own bracelets and another on advice for talking to boys.

George's magazine collection had started by accident. Two summers ago, she had noticed an old issue of *Girls' Life* in the recycling bin at the library. The word *girl* had caught her eye instantly, and she had slipped the magazine in her jacket to look at later. Another girls' magazine soon followed, this time rescued from a trash can down the block from her house. The very next weekend, she had found the denim bag at a yard sale for a quarter. It was just the size of a magazine, and had a zipper along the top. It was as if the universe had wanted her to be able to store her collection safely.

George settled on a two-page spread about FRAM-ING YOUR FACE WITH MAKEUP. George had never worn makeup, but she pored over the range of colors on the left side of the page. Her heart raced in her chest. She wondered what it would feel like to really wear lipstick. George loved to put on ChapStick. She used it all winter, whether or not her lips were really chapped, and every spring she hid the tube from Mom and wore it until it ran out.

George jumped when she heard a clatter outside. She looked out the window to the front door directly below. No one was in sight, but Scott's bike lay in the driveway, the back wheel still spinning.

Scott's bike! That meant Scott! Scott was George's older brother, a high school freshman. The hair on George's neck stood up. Soon, heavy footsteps climbed the stairs to the second floor. The locked bathroom door rattled. It was as if Scott were rattling George's heart inside her rib cage.

Bang! Bang Bang!

"You in there, George?"

"Y-yeah." The shiny magazines were spread across the tile floor. She gathered them into a pile and stuffed them into the denim bag. Her heart was thumping almost as loudly as Scott's foot against the door.

"Yo, bro, I gotta go!" Scott yelled from the far side.

George zipped up the bag as quietly as she could and looked for a place to stash it. She couldn't walk out with it. Scott would want to know what was inside. The bathroom's one cabinet was stuffed with towels and didn't shut all the way. No good either. Finally, she hung the bag from the showerhead and closed the curtain, desperately hoping that this wouldn't be the moment Scott discovered personal hygiene.

Scott rushed in as soon as George opened the door, unzipping his jeans before he reached the toilet. George exited quickly, closed the door, and leaned on the wall outside to catch her breath. The bag was probably still swinging in the shower. George hoped it wouldn't hit against the curtain or, worse, fall and land in the bathtub with a thud.

George didn't want to be standing near the bathroom when Scott came out, so she went down to the kitchen. She poured herself a glass of orange juice and sat at the table, her skin tingling. Outside, a cloud passed overhead and the room grew darker. When the bathroom door banged open, George jumped in her seat, splashing juice on her hand. She realized she had barely been breathing.

Thump, thump, thump-thump-thump-thump-thump. Scott tromped downstairs, a DVD case in his hand. He opened the refrigerator door, pulled out the carton of orange juice, and took a long swig. He wore a thin black T-shirt and jeans with a small hole in the knee. He hadn't gotten a haircut in months, and dark-brown curls formed a mop on his head.

"Sorry if I busted in on you while you were taking a dump." Scott wiped the juice off his lips with his bare forearm.

"I wasn't taking a dump," George said.

"Then what took you so long?"

George hesitated.

"Oh . . . I know," Scott said. "I'll bet you had a magazine in there."

George froze, her mouth half-open and her brain mid-thought. The air felt warm and her mind swirled. She put her hands on the table to make sure she was still there.

"That's it." Scott grinned, oblivious to George's panic. "That's my little bro! Growing up and looking at dirty magazines."

"Oh," George said out loud. She knew what dirty magazines were. She almost laughed. The girls in the magazines she was looking at wore a lot more clothes than that, even the ones at the beach. George relaxed, at least a little.

"Don't worry, George. I won't tell Mom. Anyway, I'm heading back out. Just had to get this." Scott shook the black plastic box he held in his hand, and the DVD inside rattled. "Haven't even seen it yet, but it's supposed to be a classic. It's German. The title means something like *The Blood of Evil*. When the zombies gnaw this one guy's arm off and kill him, this other guy has to use the gnawed-off arm of his dead best friend to fight the zombies. It's awesome."

"It sounds gross," George said.

"It is!" Scott nodded enthusiastically. He took another gulp of orange juice, put the carton back into the fridge, and headed for the door.

"I'll let you get back to thinking about girls," Scott joked on the way out.

George dashed up to the bathroom, rescued her bag,

and buried it deep inside her closet, under the toys and stuffed animals. She put a pile of dirty clothes on top, just in case. Then she closed the door and collapsed face-first onto her bed, her hands crossed over her head, pressing her elbows to her ears and wishing she were someone else—anyone else.

chapter II

CHARLOTTE DIES

Ms. Udell leaned against her giant desk, reading to her fourth-grade class from a tattered copy of *Charlotte's Web* by E. B. White. She wore her shiny black hair in a loose bun, and wooden earrings dangled from her long earlobes.

In her seat by the window, George couldn't listen. She couldn't think. Charlotte, the wonderful, kind spider, was gone and nothing was good. The whole book was about Charlotte saving the runt pig Wilbur, and then she goes and dies. It wasn't fair. George pushed her fists into her eyes, rubbing until rows and rows of tiny triangles twirled and twinkled brightly in the darkness.

A tear dropped onto George's book and spread into a spiderweb on the page. She breathed in carefully, trying not to make a sound. Shallow breath followed shallow breath until she was dizzy. She inhaled deeply, and as she did, she sniffled. Loudly. George heard whispers, clear in the quiet room.

"Heh, some girl is crying over a dead spider."

"That ain't no girl. That's George."

"Close enough," followed by laughter.

George didn't turn to look. She didn't need to. She knew exactly what she would see. Rick sat two rows over from George, and Jeff sat behind Rick. Jeff would be leaning forward in his seat, with his spiky hair nearly on Rick's shoulder. Rick would be leaning back in his shiny black baseball jacket. They would both be holding their hands to their mouths, halfheartedly trying to keep quiet.

Once, George and Rick had been friends, or at least friendly. In second grade, there had been a class checkers tournament, and George and Rick had been the two best players. The final match of the competition had been close, with Rick barely winning after he'd been able to king his final piece. Even though George had lost, the two had still called each other Checkers Champs for weeks.

In third grade, Jeff joined the class. Jeff had moved from California and wasn't happy about it. He started a few fistfights and threatened most of the boys at first, including George. But Jeff settled in by October, and once Jeff and Rick became buddies, Rick wasn't so friendly with George anymore. By winter break, Jeff and Rick were inseparable, and now it was as if the Checkers Champs were two kids who had known each other once, but had never met either George or Rick.

Ms. Udell glared at the snickering boys, cleared her throat, and read the final paragraph of the chapter. Her students were old enough that she rarely read aloud to them, but today she wanted them to be able to focus on what she called the "magnificent melancholy of Charlotte's final moments."

When she was finished, Ms. Udell closed the book, placed it on top of a pile of papers on her desk, and removed her glasses. "I'd like all of you to take out your journals and spend a few minutes with your reactions to this chapter. You may take a moment to reflect, but then get your pencils moving. I want you to dig deep and use some *feeling* words."

Room 205 filled with the sounds of journals being removed from desks, pages being turned, and pencils being searched for. Ms. Udell walked down the aisle toward Jeff and Rick, and spoke to them privately. Her voice blended in with the noise of the room, so George could barely hear her even though she was only two seats away.

"Some of us take death very seriously." Ms. Udell's words were icy. She looked at Jeff and Rick in turn; they each stared at their sneakers. "It is a solemn topic, and I hope that you will respect yourselves, your classmates, and life itself by treating it as such."

Jeff and Rick mumbled apologies. George wasn't sure whether their halfhearted *sorry*s were meant for her, Ms. Udell, or Charlotte. She wasn't sure she cared. The moment Ms. Udell turned away, Jeff rolled his eyes. Jeff was always rolling his eyes at something, usually with a snide comment to match.

Ms. Udell passed by George's desk. "To be honest, I'm not sure what I think of a person who doesn't cry at the end of *Charlotte's Web*."

"You didn't," George mumbled.

"I did the first three times . . . and a good number of times since." Ms. Udell paused, and for a moment it looked as if she might tear up right then. "My point is, it takes a special person to cry over a book. It shows compassion as well as imagination." Ms. Udell patted George's shoulder. "Don't ever lose that, George, and I know you'll turn into a fine young man."

The word *man* hit like a pile of rocks falling on George's skull. It was a hundred times worse than *boy*, and she couldn't breathe. She bit her lip fiercely and felt fresh tears pounding against her eyes. She put her head down on her desk and wished she were invisible.

Ms. Udell returned with the bathroom pass. It was a worn wooden block from a kindergarten class and read BOYS in thick green permanent marker on one side. George flipped the block over with a hollow *slap* so the side facing her read ROOM 205.

Ms. Udell put her hand on George's shoulder, but George shook her off and stood up. She could barely see her way to the classroom door through her tear-blurred eyes, and she navigated the hallway more from memory than sight. She stumbled, sobbing, into the bathroom— the boys' bathroom. Her lips trembled and salty tears dripped into her mouth.

George hated the boys' bathroom. It was the worst room in the school. She hated the smell of pee and bleach, and she hated the blue tiles on the wall to remind you where you were, as if the urinals didn't make it obvious enough. The whole room was about being a boy, and when boys were in there, they liked to talk about what was between their legs. George tried never to use it when there were any boys inside. She never drank from the water fountains at school, even if she was thirsty, and some days, she could make it through the school day without having to go once.

George put her head down close to the faucet and splashed cold water over her neck until she shivered. Then she rubbed a clump of paper towels on her head. She combed strings of still-wet hair with her fingers and smiled weakly at herself in the mirror.

Back in the hallway, George held the hall pass loosely in her fingers and let it drag along the wall, sending vibrations up her hand. The rhythmic *click* echoed down the hall as the wooden block skipped over the thin strips of cement between the tiles.

George opened the classroom door slowly, fearing laughter, but students were too focused on their journals to notice her return. The topic, "Personal Reactions," was written on the board in Ms. Udell's careful print. George pulled out her journal and wrote the date and the topic. By the time she had written *Charlotte is dead*, journal time was over.

Ms. Udell didn't ask anyone to read aloud. Instead, she addressed the class. "Tomorrow the real fun begins! For now, I am pleased to say that we are done for the day." She spoke the rhyme as if it were a short poem. "Put away your notebooks, and we'll see which row is ready to get its things."

By *fun*, Ms. Udell was referring to the play version of *Charlotte's Web* that the two fourth-grade classes would perform for the younger grades. It was a school tradition that each spring, every student in the first through fourth grades read the same book. The first graders had the story read to them by their teachers, and sometimes even the kindergartners participated. Every grade then did some sort of project. As the oldest students participating, the fourth graders put on a play of the book for the younger grades as well as for the parent-teacher association. Only the fifth grade wasn't involved, because they needed to focus on the spring tests to make sure they graduated and moved on to middle school.

Ms. Udell had called four rows of students, and the room was filled with the sounds of zippers and backpacks being dropped onto wooden desks. George's row was the last to be called, and the kids in it had their eyes trained on Ms. Udell.

"Row one."

Chairs screeched against the floor. George gathered her things slowly, stalling as long as she could before joining the boys' line. She wanted as much distance from Jeff and Rick as possible.

Ms. Udell's class walked through the halls of the school and down to the yard. The bus kids were released as a group, while other children waited with Ms. Udell to meet up with their parents, grandparents, or baby-sitters. George headed to her bus line.

"George, wait up!" a voice called from behind her. Kelly, George's best friend, wore her hair in braids and smelled like oranges and pencil shavings. She wore a T-shirt that read:

99% GENIUS

1% CHOCOLATE

"My dad said you could come over this weekend to practice," she said as soon as she got to George. She had been chattering about the auditions all week. "You do still want to be in the play together, right?"

George did want to be in the play. More than anything. But she didn't want to be some smelly pig. She wanted to be Charlotte, the kind and wise spider, even if it was a girl's part. Her mouth was open, but she couldn't speak.

Kelly held up her hands, palms in front of George's eyes. "I am Kelly the All-Wonderful and All-Knowing," she intoned. "I can sense that you are not well. Now, my child, what seems to be your problem?" She closed her eyes and slowly brought her hands to the sides of George's head, peeking just a little bit to make sure she didn't poke her best friend in the eye.

"If you're all-knowing, then don't you already know?" George asked.

Kelly opened her eyes long enough to cross them so that they pointed at her nose. Then she fluttered her eyelids shut.

"Fine. I am Kelly the All-Wonderful and Mostly Knowing. I will try to sense your problem." She opened her eyes again and dropped her hands. "I know! You've got stage fright. I know all about stage fright. My uncle

Bill says my dad has terrible stage fright and that's why he lets other people get rich performing his songs."

"It's not stage fright."

"Okay, maybe not. I don't think my dad has stage fright either. He's just a different kind of artist." Kelly shook George's shoulder. "But then, what *is* it? You *know* I can't handle suspense. Tell me or I'll . . ."

"Or you'll what?"

Kelly's eyes gleamed with inspiration. "Or I'll bring out my army of beasts to attack you in the night, and suck out your brains with a crazy straw, and make you one of my minions so you have to do everything I say. Including telling me what you're thinking about! What is it? What is it? What is it?"

George looked around to make sure no one else could hear.

"Okay, okay, calm down! Here's the thing. I don't really want to be *Wilbur* in the play," she told Kelly.

"Oh. That's not a problem. There are a lot of other parts in the play. They're called supporting roles. My dad says the best star performers would be nothing without an excellent supporting cast. Let Ms. Udell hear you and decide what part you should have."

"I don't want just any part," said George.

"Well, who do you want to be? Templeton the rat?"

George shook her head.

"Avery?" Kelly guessed. "Mr. Zuckerman? Mr. Arable?"

George still shook her head.

"Who else is there?" Kelly asked incredulously.

"I want to be Charlotte," George whispered.

Kelly shrugged. "That's cool. If you want to be Charlotte, you should try out for Charlotte. You make such a big deal out of everything. Who cares if you're not really a girl?"

George's stomach dropped. She cared. Tons.

On the street, one of the buses started its engine.

"I gotta go!" Kelly broke into a run. "One-two-three!" she called behind her.

"Zoot," George replied. Back in first grade, Kelly and George had decided that saying *one-two-three-zoot* was a lot more fun than saying *good-bye*. They had heard it on a cartoon, and it had made them laugh all day. Neither of them could remember anymore what show it was from, and sometimes it seemed silly to still be saying *one-two-three-zoot*, but neither wanted to be the first one to stop.

● ● ●

That night, George dreamed she was onstage as Charlotte. She wore all black, with extra limbs running down her sides, and she recited the most beautiful words for the entire auditorium to hear. Her first line was delivered perfectly, as was the second. But then there was a strange noise overhead. George looked up, but all she could see was the heavy stage curtain, which enveloped her in a stuffy darkness before knocking her off the ladder. Then she was falling and couldn't breathe for what felt like a very long time.

George woke up in a sweat. It took a moment to realize she was awake, in her bed, and not suffocating. Her bedsheet was twisted around her legs.

Still, she couldn't shake the image of being Charlotte. As she ate her cereal and milk, as she dressed in jeans and a T-shirt, as she brushed her teeth, she pictured herself greeting the audience with a fine "Salutations." She should be the one to declare Wilbur *terrific*. And she should be the one to make people cry with her final farewell.

chapter III

ACTING IS JUST PRETEND

George lived in the left side of a two-unit house with Mom and Scott. When George referred to her family, Mom and Scott were usually who she meant. Dad lived with his new wife, Fiona, in a house in the Pennsylvania Pocono Mountains, a few hours away. Scott and George visited every summer for two weeks, like sleepaway camp. Dad made a better part-time father than a full-time one.

Mr. and Mrs. Williams lived in the other half of the house. They were a retired couple whose adventures outdoors generally consisted of a daily slipper-clad shuffle to pick up the mail and newspaper. George found them calm and likable, and hoped they never moved away. If a new family moved in next door, they might have a boy her age. Then Mom would expect George and the boy to be best friends.

You two will have so much fun, Mom would say. *Just introduce yourself and smile.* Mom was smart, and George loved her a lot, but Mom didn't know about boys. Boys didn't like George, and George wasn't so sure what she thought about them, either.

George walked her bike from the shed in the backyard, along the cracked cement path, and up to the street. It was Sunday afternoon, and Kelly had invited her over to practice for Monday's auditions. Kelly said they could take turns playing Charlotte, and George's stomach danced at the idea of reading the spider's words aloud. George biked to Kelly's house, her short afternoon shadow leading the way down the main road.

Kelly and her father lived in a two-room basement

apartment, and their front door was really a back door. The backyard was more pavement than grass, though tufts of green sprouted eagerly through cracks in the concrete.

George propped her bike against the back wall of the house, hung her helmet from the handlebar, and guided herself down the three treacherously steep concrete steps, holding on to the thin metal railing for support. She knocked hard on the wooden door to compete with the rock music blasting inside.

Kelly greeted her with a giant smile. The apartment opened directly into a large, messy room. Kitchen appliances and a sink full of dishes lined one wall. In another corner sat an unmade daybed. Cardboard boxes were stashed everywhere. Piles of books and papers were stacked up wherever they would fit: on the desk, on the bookcases, in shoe boxes above the bookcases, on top of the TV, pouring out of the open closet. George had even seen sheet music peeking out of the freezer a few times.

(Kelly had said that was for when her dad needed to let a piece of music cool down before he could work on it some more.) A single standing lamp attempted to light the room, but the corners of the apartment were encased in shadows.

Kelly's father was a musician, but he didn't play onstage very often. Instead, he wrote music for other people to perform. Kelly swore the people her dad had written for were famous, but George never recognized their names. When Kelly came over to George's for dinner, she loved to rattle off the singers and bands to George's mom, who recognized a few.

Today, Kelly's father sat in the middle of the floor, his eyes intent on the paper in his hands. He was surrounded by dozens of stacks of sheet music stretching across the room, both loose and bound into books. Some of the stacks were over two feet tall. He added the page he was holding to a pile behind him that looked ready to topple.

"My dad's cleaning!" Kelly announced. "What do you think?"

"Wow," said George. That seemed to cover the extent of the damage.

"Got to mess it up before you can fix it up," Kelly's dad yelled over the music. He picked his way over to the stereo to turn down the volume. "Hey, George."

"Hey." George never knew what to call Kelly's father. *Mr. Arden* was too formal for a person like him, but George felt funny calling an adult by his first name, even though he had said "Call me Paul" more than once. To George, he was just Kelly's dad, but she didn't think he really wanted to be called that.

"So, you here to be a big-time actor?" he asked as he lifted a box off a pile and added it to the mess on the ground.

"I guess so," said George.

"C'mon, let's get started." Kelly took George by the

hand and walked her across the stained beige carpet to the door of her room. "Have fun with your project, Dad. Knock if you need us. And try to keep it down. We've got lines to rehearse, and you know how important those are."

"Yes, ma'am!" Kelly's dad gave a firm nod and returned his attention to the next piece of sheet music on the pile in front of him.

Walking inside Kelly's room was like entering another world. The desk and bureau were spotless, her bed was neatly made, and dozens of framed photographs hung stylishly on the walls. Fresh vacuum lines streaked across the rose-pink carpeting, and the air smelled like lemons.

"Wow, Kelly. Your room's even neater than usual."

"I went on a cleaning binge. It's what inspired my dad."

"Maybe you should give him lessons."

"Ha! He thinks finding lost stuff is half the fun. He says it's like digging for gold. Anyway, I think you've got a great idea."

"What idea?"

"Trying out for Charlotte. Ms. Udell will love that you care so much about the character that you want to play her onstage, even though she's a girl and you're a boy. Plays are all about pretending, right?"

"Um . . ." was all George could say. Playing a girl part wouldn't really be pretending, but George didn't know how to tell Kelly that. Besides, it was hard to stop Kelly once she got started. Mom said that Kelly should be a lawyer. Kelly said her dad would sue her if she tried.

"You know," Kelly continued, "she'll probably give you the part just to make the point. She's always going on about how we're not supposed to let people's expectations limit our choices."

"But it's more than just the play," George tried to explain.

"Of course it is. There's a whole history of boys playing girls in *thee-ay-trah*. Did you know that all the characters in Shakespeare's plays were played by men? Even the girl parts. Even when they had to kiss! Can you believe it?"

George thought for a moment about kissing a boy, and the idea made her tingle. Living in Shakespeare's time didn't sound so bad, even if you had to poop outdoors.

Kelly went on. "Romeo and Juliet were both played by boys. Boys! Just think. William Shakespeare himself might have played Juliet. If you want to be Charlotte, you should get to try out, like anyone else. It's only fair. And if you get nervous, my dad says you just have to picture the audience naked."

George didn't see how that would help. "Kelly?" she said.

"Yeah?"

"Your dad is weird."

"I know *that*."

Kelly stood in the center of the room and took a few bows, as if she were onstage. She looked around nervously and then pointed at her imaginary audience, yelling, "How can I act in front of you people? You're all naked! This is extremely rude!"

Kelly started to giggle, and George joined her until the two of them curled into howling balls of laughter, occasionally shouting things like "I can't perform under these conditions!", "Where's my limo?", and "Get me my agent!" until finally, winded and with sore cheeks, their chuckles grew further apart. Suddenly, Kelly jumped up, determination in her face.

"Okay, let's get to work." She opened the bottom drawer of her desk. Inside, a rainbow of hanging file folders kept numerous papers in place. Kelly took a pair of pages from a file in the front, then rolled the drawer shut.

"I made a copy on my dad's printer last night." Kelly thrust a page at George. The word **CHARLOTTE** stood in capital letters at the top, originally written with a thick marker. Below it was the first conversation between Charlotte and Wilbur. All of the girls, no matter what part they wanted, would be auditioning with Charlotte's lines, and the boys would be auditioning with Wilbur's.

"Why don't you play Charlotte first?" Kelly dropped to her hands and knees, laying her script on the carpet in front of her.

She oinked up at George, who perched herself as high as she could on the pillows at the head of the bed. As they acted out the scene, George surprised herself. She thought she would be nervous, but it seemed natural to say Charlotte's words aloud. They were finished too quickly.

"Switch places!" Kelly called, flopping onto the bed and lying on her back with her head hanging off the side. She held the paper out at arm's length in front of her, upside down so she could read it. "Ready," she called.

George climbed off the bed and sat cross-legged on the floor. She read Wilbur's lines and heard Kelly echo back the words she had read aloud moments ago. George was delighted when it was time to switch back. She climbed majestically up to the peak of the bed, stretching her limbs out like a spider's, while Kelly jumped onto the floor and snorted.

"Salutations!" George cried, and the scene began again. The words felt good on her lips.

The two friends ran the dialogue back and forth until they could say most of the lines without looking at the page. Eventually, Kelly refused to give up her spot as Wilbur, and George happily repeated the role of Charlotte.

"You don't mind?" asked George. She could have read Charlotte's words all day long.

"I'm having fun!" Kelly said. "Besides, you make a better Charlotte than I do. I keep goofing up the first line!"

Kelly was right. She kept saying "Sa-lu-ta-TA-tions" instead of "Sal-u-TA-tions." *Salutations* was the fancy way Charlotte first greeted Wilbur and showed off her magnificent vocabulary. It was an important first line.

"There are other parts. I could be Fern. I'll be all 'Pa! Where are you going with that ax?'" She held up her hands in imaginary protest.

"Ax? What ax?" Kelly's father had opened the door and popped his head in. "I ain't got no ax. I'm strictly a bass man. *Da-dum-dum-dum-dum-dum.*" He slapped his fingers against his waist, playing an imaginary instrument. "Get it? Ax? Bass?"

"Really, Dad?" Kelly gave her father a look. George smiled blankly.

Kelly turned to George. "Hotshot lead guitarists like to call their guitars *axes*. It makes them think they're cool." She refocused her attention on her father. "Didn't I tell you to knock first? We're trying to rehearse."

"You've been at it a while. I thought you might be thirsty. There's white grape juice in the fridge."

"Well, in that case, my dear father," Kelly proclaimed, "I don't mind you bothering us at all. Why, with all this rehearsing, I'm downright parched."

"I'll bet your co-star is too, Ms. Arden. What do you say, Mr. Mitchell? Care for a beverage?"

George nodded. She hated being called Mr. Mitchell. She wanted to shout, *Mr. Mitchell lives in the Poconos with a woman named Fiona!* Mr. Mitchell was her dad's name. It would be her brother Scott's name someday too, but it would never be hers.

Instead, George followed Kelly into the main room of the apartment and over to the fridge, where Kelly poured juice into two plastic cups that had come from a local barbecue shack. Most of the dishes in the cabinets were made of plastic. There were a few real glasses at the back of the shelf, the remnants of several different sets, but no one ever seemed to use them. Given how often cups were knocked over in the Arden home, this was probably a good idea.

Kelly gulped her juice down in three swallows. "Ahhhhhhhhhhh! White grape juice. My favorite!" She wiped her hand across her mouth, added the cup to the pile of dishes filling the sink, and set herself in the empty space on the floor where her father had been sitting among a chaos of paper. She oinked several times and pushed the nearest piles carefully out of her way before rolling onto her back and rocking back and forth, a pig gleefully wallowing in mud.

Kelly's father snatched her cup from the top of the dish pile and poured a glass of grape juice for himself. He chuckled at his daughter's antics.

"Are you trying to say that my room is a pigsty?"

Kelly oinked and nodded vigorously.

Kelly's dad turned to George. "Care to stay for dinner? I'm making *Super Special Surprise!*"

"Um, thanks, but I think my mom wants me home."

"As you wish."

Kelly took her best friend by the hand and escorted her back to her room. They ran through their lines once more. George would have liked to play the role of Charlotte all day long, but Kelly declared boredom and pulled out her camera.

The camera was small and silver, with a lens in the front that zoomed in and out. She had gotten it for her birthday last summer, and there hadn't been a day since that she hadn't taken a picture of something. She loved framing the shot—deciding just where the picture should start and what should stay unseen.

Some of the photographs on her walls were portraits. One of Kelly's dad onstage playing his bass. Another of her uncle Bill painting in a field of dandelions like a hippie. And a grainy photo of a tall, dark-skinned woman in heels and a shiny blue dress, holding a microphone. It was the only picture on the wall that Kelly hadn't taken herself, and while she almost never talked about it, George knew it was a photo of Kelly's mom.

Not all of the pictures were of people Kelly knew, though. There was a kid smiling on the monkey bars, a man in a suit drinking coffee while deep in thought, and an old couple holding hands on a park bench. Other photographs were images of everyday objects so close up that you could barely tell what they were anymore. There was a worn-down pencil eraser, a pile of Q-tips, the strings of a guitar, and a shadowy shape with a shimmering silver triangle in the middle. Even Kelly didn't remember what that object had originally been, but it was George's favorite.

Kelly directed George to stand against the back of her door and began to shoot.

"Put your left foot in front of your right," she told George. George did, but Kelly frowned. "Nah, put it back." She took a few more shots. "Look up in the sky. No, not like you're looking at a plane. Like you're looking at a leaf on a tree."

George didn't mind so much when Kelly took a few pictures of her, but she hated it when Kelly tried to pose her. Kelly was persistent, though, and it was faster to let her take her pictures than to argue with her, lose, and have Kelly take even more shots to prove her point.

Kelly modeled George with a book, and shot close-ups of the spaces between her fingers. She gave George a baseball cap and sunglasses to wear and took pictures until George couldn't take it anymore and begged her to stop.

"What if we take some outside?" Kelly asked.

"Nah," George replied. "I gotta get home."

"Fine. Anyway, you better go before my dad announces that *Super Special Surprise* is ready and insists that you stay."

"What is *Super Special Surprise*, anyway?"

"My dad fries up a bunch of leftovers. Occasionally, it's awesome. Usually, it's so-so. And sometimes, it's so bad we have to order pizza."

George said good-bye to Kelly and walked her bike up the cracked path along the house. "One-two-three—" Kelly called out from the basement window.

"ZOOT!" George yelled into the early evening air. She strapped on her helmet and began the familiar ride home. Houses passed by in a blur while Charlotte's words continued to roll through her mind.

● ● ●

At home, Mom was staring at the open pantry cabinet, her long, dark-brown hair back in its usual ponytail. She wore a polo shirt and blue jeans—the same clothes she wore under her white lab coat at work every day. She preferred jeans to skirts and didn't wear makeup. She said it wasn't good for your skin, and, besides, women were beautiful enough the way they were. Indeed,

Mom was beautiful. She was tall, with a kind, genuine smile, and had the same bright-green eyes as George.

"Hey, Gee-gee," she said as she shut the pantry door.

When George was little and couldn't say her name properly, she used to call herself Gee-gee. Mom still called her that, even though Scott said that it sounded like a girl's name. George secretly thought the same thing.

"Have you seen your brother?" Mom asked as she rustled through the fridge for dinner options.

"He went to Randy's house."

"Hot dogs and beans it is!"

Scott hated baked beans, but both George and her mother loved them.

While Mom made dinner, George headed upstairs to take a bath. She took off her shirt while the tub filled, waiting until the last possible moment to take off her pants and underwear. She immersed her body in the warm water and tried not to think about what was between her legs, but there it was, bobbing in front of her. She washed her hair with lots of shampoo so that the suds would cover the surface of the water. She scrubbed her body, stood with a splash, and dried off with her fuzzy blue towel. Then she wrapped the towel around her torso, up by her armpits the way girls do, and ran a small black comb through her hair. She brushed it forward and stared at her pale, freckled face in the mirror before combing it back into its regular part down the middle.

In her room, George changed into a pair of flannel pajamas covered in tiny penguins wearing red bow ties. Mom called that dinner was ready, and George went downstairs to eat.

Mom already sat at the kitchen table, getting ready to take a bite of her hot dog, which was covered in mustard and relish. She had toasted her bun but had left George's soft and cool, just the way she liked it.

"Thanks, Mom," said George. She squirted some ketchup onto her hot dog and took a steaming, juicy bite.

They ate in silence at first. Scott was usually the one who talked the most at dinner. But a question was burning in George's mind. Over and over it played.

"Mom?" she said after she swallowed the last bite of her hot dog. She barely realized she had spoken aloud.

"What's up, Gee-gee?"

George stopped. It was such a short, little question, but she couldn't make her mouth form the sounds.

Mom, what if I'm a girl?

George had seen an interview on television a few months ago with a beautiful woman named Tina. She had golden-brown skin, thick hair with blond highlights, and long, sparkling fingernails. The interviewer said that Tina had been born a boy, then asked her whether she'd had *the surgery*. The woman replied that she was a *transgender woman* and that what she had between her legs was nobody's business but hers and her boyfriend's.

So George knew it could be done. A boy could become a girl. She had since read on the Internet that you could take girl hormones that would change your body, and you could get a bunch of different surgeries if you wanted them and had the money. This was called *transitioning*. You could even start before you were eighteen with pills called androgen blockers that stopped the boy hormones already inside you from turning your body into a man's. But for that, you needed your parents' permission.

"George, whatever it is, you can tell me." Mom took George's hand in one of her own, and covered it with the other. "Whatever happens in your life, you can share it, and I will love you. You will always be my little boy, and that will never change. Even when you grow up to be an old man, I will still love you as my son."

George opened her lips, but there were no words in her mouth and only one thought in her brain: *No!*

George knew that Mom was trying to help. But George didn't have a normal problem. She wasn't scared of snakes. She hadn't failed a math test. She was a girl, and no one knew it.

"Mom, could I have some chocolate milk?"

"Oh, Gee-gee, of course." She went to the fridge.

In the weeks after Dad had left the house, Mom had given George a glass of chocolate milk every night before bed. Neither of them would say anything. Neither of them had anything to say. But these were some of George's favorite memories, just sitting there, being with Mom, knowing she would never leave.

George wouldn't finish her chocolate milk until she was ready for Mom to kiss her good night. Then Mom would take the nearly empty glass and turn it over above her mouth for one last drop. George always made sure to leave that last thick sip.

Now Mom came back to the table with a full glass of chocolate milk, frothy from a fresh stirring. The sweetness filled George's mouth. She focused her eyes firmly on the creamy bubbles, now resting halfway down the glass.

She stared at the foam for a minute, and then downed the second half. She felt more than tasted it, coldness running down her throat. Then she handed the glass to Mom, who tipped it over her tongue for that final drop.

The sweetness of the chocolate milk had coated George's tongue, covering the words sitting on its tip. Someday, somehow, George would have to tell Mom that she was a girl. But this was not that day.

And as for how, she had no idea.

chapter IV

ANTICIPATION

The students of Room 205 tromped up the cold, dark stone stairs. Their footfalls echoed heavily off the tile walls. Two handrails ran along either side of the wall, one a foot above the other. They had been painted red years ago but had chipped over time, revealing layers of orange and green, and patches of bare steel underneath. The girls walked up with handrails on their right. The boys had handrails on their left, and they traveled the long way around the platform halfway up the flight.

Bulletin boards on the second floor were lined with construction-paper Wilburs and Charlottes that the younger grades had decorated. Principal Maldonado stood at the far end of the hallway. She watched without a word or a smile, making sure the classes filed quietly into their rooms, where teachers sat with lesson plans on their cluttered desks and assignments on the whiteboards.

In Room 205, the morning journal assignment was written in neat script on the board. It read *If you could be a color, what color would you want to be? Explain why in no less than 5 lines.* The class settled into the rhythm of the morning, and scratches of pencils in notebooks replaced the metallic scrapes of chairs and coat zippers.

Once the line at the pencil sharpener had faded and most students were finished writing, Ms. Udell called on a few volunteers to read their journal entries. Janelle said she would be fuchsia because it was bright and dark at the same time. Chris wanted to be orange because it was the only color that was a food.

George wanted to be pink so that people would know she was a girl, but she hadn't written that down.

Instead, she'd said she wanted to be purple, like the sky at sunrise. She didn't raise her hand to read her journal aloud. She never did. Ms. Udell said that it was okay for journals to be private.

At the end of journal time, Ms. Udell addressed the class. "I know this is a big day that many of you have been waiting for—perhaps even *rehearsing* for." Murmurs filled the room, as well as a few giggles from the girls. George felt a warm wave pass over her as she remembered reading Charlotte's lines.

"I am happy to announce that I will be holding try-outs at one thirty," Ms. Udell continued. The class groaned. That was hours away. "Anyone who is caught looking at his or her lines instead of paying attention today, as well as anyone who asks me questions about the audition before one thirty this afternoon"—Ms. Udell paused for effect—"will be deemed unable to handle the *responsibility* of performing."

She nodded her head firmly, indicating that she had finished with the topic. The class waded through a morning of math, reading, and science, wishing impatiently for the afternoon to arrive.

● ● ●

"Who eats green beans with spaghetti?" Kelly winced as she dropped her orange tray onto the long table. The school lunchroom was in the basement, and the grated windows near the tops of the tile walls let in little light. Most of the illumination in the large room came from long fluorescent bulbs that ran along the high ceiling.

George was already sitting down, poking at mushy strands of vegetable with her spork. She leaned down to sniff them, but couldn't smell anything other than the faint scent of spoiled milk that had seeped deep into the lunch table and couldn't be removed with all the bleach in the world.

"Who eats green beans with anything?" George asked, crinkling her nose.

"I happen to love green beans, you know. When my dad sautés them in garlic with just a touch of olive oil . . ." Kelly brought her fingers to her mouth and kissed them to the air. *"Mmm-wa! Bon appétit!* But this stuff?" She picked up a droopy bean between her thumb and forefinger. "It's limper than the spaghetti! Which is overdone too! It's not al dente, which is how you're supposed to cook pasta. *Al dente* is Italian for 'to the tooth' and it means it's still a little hard in the center, so you have to actually chew it." Kelly picked up a few strands of spaghetti on her spork and wiggled them in the air. "This stuff is not al dente. I can tell you that much."

George shrugged and spun her spork to gather up a mouthful of spaghetti. The lunchroom was already noisy, and getting louder as the rest of the third- through fifth-grade classes filed through the lunch lines and filled the long tables.

"So do you want to practice?" Kelly asked.

"Not here." George nodded at the crowded table. She didn't want anyone else in the class to hear her reciting Charlotte's lines.

"You know they'll find out when you get the part," Kelly pointed out.

"That's different . . . *if* I get it." George wasn't sure exactly how it would be different, so she tried not to think about it.

"Whatever. We'll practice during recess."

Kelly snuck her camera out of her pocket to take pictures of the limp beans and spaghetti until Mrs. Fields, the lunchtime volunteer, scrunched her face in Kelly's direction and told her to put the camera away.

"Artists are never appreciated at lunchtime," Kelly mumbled as she stuffed her camera into her pocket.

Outside, the smell of pine trees wafted in from the yards of the houses that bordered the back of the school. The air was filled with the buzz of a hundred students at recess, punctuated by yells, laughter, and, occasionally, Mrs. Fields's piercing whistle. She was a short, wrinkly prune of a woman with poofy gray hair who disapproved of everything and walked with a hunched back that made her look even shorter and wrinklier than she already was.

Maddy, Emma, and several other girls were gathered in a circle, gossiping about their favorite television show, *Not-So-Plain Jane*, and whether their parents would let them go next month to see Jane Plane, star of the show, live in concert.

Jeff had a circle of kids around him too, hoping to get a turn to see his new phone. Mrs. Fields would confiscate it if she saw it, so the boys around him huddled in close. Jeff didn't let any of them hold it, but he allowed a chosen few to touch the screen.

Kelly and George found a quiet spot at the far end of the fence to practice. Kelly pulled a copy of the script page out of her pocket. George knew her lines and didn't need to look at the sheet once as she spoke, but her heart thumped heavily and she spoke too quickly, swallowing the final words of each line. She glanced behind her whenever Kelly spoke, to make sure no one was watching, and missed half her cues.

Kelly frowned when they were done. "That wasn't your best performance."

"I know."

"Do you want to run through it again?"

"No!" A few nearby third graders turned their heads in the direction of George's shout. She lowered her voice. "I mean, no. It's too open. I'll be all right when I'm alone with Ms. Udell."

"I still don't see what the big deal is," Kelly said. "So

you want to play a girl onstage. It's not like you want to *be* a girl."

George's face paled. The air grew hot around her.

"What's wrong?" Kelly asked.

George opened her mouth, but there were no words, so she closed it again. She started to giggle nervously. George's charged laughter filled the air, and soon, Kelly was chuckling too, though she didn't know why. George's laughter grew frantic, and she felt light-headed. Her knees buckled and she dropped to the ground. Not wanting to feel left out, Kelly fell to the black pavement as well.

The kids in the yard ignored George and Kelly, but Mrs. Fields didn't.

"Off the ground!" she commanded. "You don't know what animals have urinated there!"

Kelly jumped up and extended a hand to George, who took it and let Kelly pull her to her feet.

"I hope an animal urinates on her head," Kelly whispered to George. Then she asked, "So . . . what were we laughing about?"

George stared at her best friend. "Are you serious?"

"Of course I'm serious," Kelly said, the bright sun shining on her earnest face. "I'm always serious. Except, you know, when I'm not serious. But right now I'm serious."

"But you *said* it!" George didn't know whether to be relieved or upset that Kelly didn't see that she was a girl. The high pitch in her voice revealed her anxiety.

"All I said was . . ." Kelly paused. "What *did* I say, George? I mean, I've always thought of myself as a funny person, but I didn't think I was such a good comedian that I could say something that funny without knowing it."

George opened her mouth, but as with Mom, she couldn't say the only words that blared through her brain: *I'm a girl.* She wished the bell ending recess would ring.

"Are you nervous about the audition?" Kelly asked. "Don't be. My dad says that men performing in non-traditional gender roles is good for feminism. He says it's important, as an artist, to be in touch with his feminine side."

Last summer, George had seen that phrase in one of her own dad's magazines, an article called 10 WAYS TO GET IN TOUCH WITH YOUR FEMININE SIDE. George had been excited to read it, but the article had been disappointing. It talked about taking time to feel your emotions, which George did too much already. Worse, the article kept reminding the reader that finding your *feminine* side made you more of a man.

"Can we not talk about it anymore?" George asked. Somehow, it was worse that Kelly thought it was no big deal that George wanted to be Charlotte in the play than if she had said it was a terrible idea. It was as if Kelly didn't see that anything was wrong at all.

"Criminy, you're like a safe, you are!"

"What?"

Kelly shrugged. "I don't know. My dad says it."

"Kelly." George took Kelly by the shoulders, ignored the tickle in her stomach, and spoke very seriously. "In case you hadn't noticed, your dad is still weird."

Deep inside, George worried that she was even weirder.

chapter V

AUDITIONS

After lunch, the class plodded through a spelling pretest, followed by a science work sheet on simple machines, but all George could think about was trying out for Charlotte. Maybe Kelly was right and Ms. Udell would be so proud of George for being herself that she would give her the part. The minute hand of the clock was a terribly slow lever, pushing the hour hand imperceptibly forward.

Finally, Mrs. Fields's wrinkled knuckles rapped on the heavy glass window of the classroom door. Ms. Udell welcomed her in. She would be watching the class while

Ms. Udell auditioned students in the hallway. Outside of the lunchroom, she smelled like Necco candy wafers.

"I congratulate you all for your patience." Ms. Udell looked directly at Kelly and winked. "The time has finally come to see how you fare as actors and actresses. Everyone who auditions will be given a part."

Ms. Udell would be auditioning students from both Room 205 and Mr. Jackson's fourth-grade class in Room 207. Half of the roles would go to students from each class. Ms. Udell pushed her clunky wooden chair toward the classroom door.

"Today, you are each reading Charlotte's or Wilbur's lines, but I am also casting for Fern, Templeton, and the other characters. If you do not audition today, you will not be cast in the play. If you'd rather not be onstage, don't worry. Mr. Jackson will need quality hands on the crew."

"I was really worried," Jeff muttered.

"Mrs. Fields." Ms. Udell turned her attention to the small woman, who had pulled over a spare chair and settled herself quite comfortably at Ms. Udell's desk. "Thank you again for staying late. I do appreciate it."

"Anything for the theater."

"Please do let me know if there's anyone you find is not *mature* enough to participate in our production. I'm sure I can find other accommodations for them."

"The kitchen staff can always use a young set of scrubbin' hands," Mrs. Fields declared.

Ms. Udell returned her attention to her class and waved a stack of colored index cards. "If you are interested in trying out, I will give you a card with a number on it. The number will dictate the order of your audition. Girls first, then boys. I do not expect you to have the lines memorized, but I do expect you to deliver them clearly and with enthusiasm. You will read only your part. I will read the lines of the other characters. While you wait, you may *silently* review your part. If you do not wish to practice, you may begin your homework assignment."

Ms. Udell asked the boys who wished to audition to raise their hands. George joined them, lifting her hand just to the height of her head. Ms. Udell counted six blue index cards, shuffled them, and passed them out, along with six fresh copies of the practice part. George was number six. Last. The longest to possibly wait until her audition, with **WILBUR** staring up at her in bold, thick letters. George slumped in her chair and turned the page over.

Ms. Udell then distributed nine pink cards to girls who raised outstretched fingers and mouthed numbers to each other.

"Yes!" exclaimed Kelly, who waved two fingers in the air at George like a victory sign.

Janelle stood, waving a card with the number one on it. She held the door open for Ms. Udell, who pushed her chair into the hallway, where they both disappeared.

George listened closely, but she couldn't hear a sound from the hallway over the murmurs and rustling papers inside the classroom.

George tried to bury her mind in her homework. Monday night's homework always took forever, because the spelling words were also vocabulary words, and Ms. Udell insisted that each student write an official dictionary definition of each word before using it in a sentence. With Mrs. Fields's permission, George headed to the back of the room.

As she bent down to get a dictionary, someone in the room sniffled. George's stomach lurched when there was another sniffle and a snort, followed by the words, "Oh, Charlotte, I miss you so," and snickers. George bit her lower lip and walked the long way back to her seat, to stay as far from Jeff's and Rick's desks as possible.

By the time George was back in her chair, Janelle popped her head in through the doorway. Kelly bounced up and rushed out the door. Soon, she came beaming back into the classroom and announced, with great flourish, "Number three, you're up!"

Kelly gave George a thumbs-up sign and hunched over in her seat. A few minutes later, on her way to pick up a dictionary from the back of the room, she dropped a note on George's desk. It was folded into a small square. When George opened it, the folds formed a grid across the page. The note read:

Charlotte,
You'll be R-A-D-I-A-N-T!!
Kelly

George couldn't help but grin. *Radiant* was one of the words Charlotte had woven into her web to save Wilbur, and it had been one of their vocabulary words last week. It meant "beaming and sparkling," and George couldn't think of a finer compliment. She took a break from her homework to recite her lines silently.

She remembered them all, and she knew just when to pause to give the words their best effect.

Maddy looked pale when she left the room, and even paler when she came back. Emma clutched her lines tightly. Maybe if the girls were terrible enough, Ms. Udell would be so relieved that George was good that she wouldn't care that George wasn't a girl. At least, not a regular girl.

There was a long wait after the last girl came back into the room, as Ms. Udell listened to the students from Mr. Jackson's class. Eventually, Ms. Udell came in to announce that it was time for the boys to take their turns. Robert was first and came back bragging, "Beat that, number two!" But George wasn't worried about the boys. Her competition was already back in their seats, writing definitions for words like *gesture* and *narrator*.

Finally, the fifth boy, Chris, went out into the hallway. He was a chubby white kid with a toothy grin. He returned with a smile wider than ever, and danced victoriously back to his seat. Then it was George's turn.

In the hallway, Ms. Udell sat in the blocky wooden chair—the one that matched her blocky wooden desk. The chair looked awkward without its mate.

"You don't have your sheet, George," Ms. Udell said.

"Don't need it."

"Well, that's a good sign. It means you must have practiced." Ms. Udell gave a kind smile. "But do speak up."

Before Ms. Udell could say anything else, George closed her eyes and began. The first words rushed out of her mouth, but then she slowed into the cadence she had practiced. She felt herself as Charlotte and gave each word her full attention as it left her tongue. The words felt even more like hers than they had in Kelly's room. George reached the end of Charlotte's monologue and was ready for the dialogue with Wilbur that followed. But George didn't hear her cue. She opened her eyes. Ms. Udell was frowning, and a thick crease had formed across her forehead.

"George, what was that?" she asked.

"I . . . ," started George, but there were no words to finish the sentence. "I . . ."

"Was that supposed to be some kind of joke? Because it wasn't very funny."

"It wasn't a joke. I want to be Charlotte." George's voice sounded much smaller now that she was speaking her own words.

"You know I can't very well cast you as Charlotte. I have too many girls who want the part. Besides, imagine how confused people would be. Now, if you're interested in being Wilbur, that's a possibility. Or maybe Templeton—he's a funny guy."

"No, thanks. I just . . . I wanted . . ."

"Okay, then." Ms. Udell eyed George oddly. "For now, we need to get into the room to get ready to go. Would you hold the door for me?"

Ms. Udell pushed her chair back into the classroom, shaking her head. She announced that it was time to pack up, and sent George's row first to the coat closet.

George muttered to herself as she loaded her math book into her bag. *Stupid stupid stupid. Stupid. Stupid body. Stupid brain. Stupid boys and stupid girls. Stupid everything.* She kicked at the leg of her desk, knocking it into Emma's chair in front of her. Emma turned back to give George a dirty look.

George stared intently at the speckled tile floor and wished she were home in her bed. When Ms. Udell called her row, George hoisted her bag onto her back and shuffled over to the boys' line, still staring at the ground.

In the yard, Kelly bounded up to George, her ponytail flopping behind her. "So? How did it go? What did she think? Was she impressed or what? I bet she'll let you be Charlotte."

"I don't want to talk about it." George scraped her foot against the pavement.

"What happened?" Kelly cried, grabbing George by the shoulders. "Did you mess up?"

"Leave me alone." George jerked back and tried to head to her bus.

"Did she not like it?"

"No, Kelly. She didn't like it. She hated it."

"She said that?!" Kelly's eyes were wide.

"She thought it was a joke."

"Oh, well. At least you tried." Kelly shrugged. "That's what my dad says."

"AAAAAAHHHH!" George screamed in Kelly's face. "I don't want to hear what your dad says!"

Kelly's shoulders shrank. She opened and closed her mouth, then turned toward her bus line.

George took the steep steps onto her own bus and shuffled along the narrow corridor, her feet sticking to the rubbery floor. She picked an empty seat midway back and hoped that no one would take the spot next to her. Hugging her backpack tightly, she buried her head in the dark space between the backpack and her chest and held back her tears.

● ● ●

"So how were tryouts?" Mom asked later that evening. She had just gotten home from work a few minutes before and had started on dinner by dumping a brick of frozen peas into a glass bowl.

"I didn't audition," George mumbled. She sat at the kitchen table, tapping her pencil on her pinkie. Early evening light fell through the window onto her fractions homework.

"Why not? You practiced with Kelly for hours on Sunday."

"There was a lot to memorize."

"Gee-gee, you know every word to every commercial that comes on TV." She pulled a bag of frozen fish fillets from the packed freezer and arranged six on a baking sheet.

George shrugged. "That's different."

"I was just so excited to see my little guy onstage." Mom tousled George's hair. George brushed her aside with a shrug and buried her head deep in her homework. Neither of them said another word until Scott slammed the front door, announcing his arrival.

"Wash up," Mom told him. "Dinner's almost ready."

"Wash up? What makes you think I'm dirty?"

"Because I've met you. You're always dirty. Now go wash your hands. With soap!"

Over dinner, Mom asked Scott about his day at school.

"It was awesome!" Scott exclaimed.

"Oh, really?" Mom was skeptical. Scott rarely showed such enthusiasm about his education. "What happened?"

"So we were in PE, you know, and we had to go to the outside track and run a mile. And I have PE sixth period, right?" Scott waved his fork around as he spoke. "So there was this kid. He's not even out of shape, really. But I think he has lunch fifth period. And I *know* he had macaroni, because he ralphed it up, all over the track. Mr. Phillips had to blow the whistle and let us stop early because he was afraid that someone would slip and fall in it."

Mom started rubbing her temples at the mention of *macaroni*, and by this point had her head fully in her hands. "Scott," she warned through tight lips.

Scott ignored her. "I was right behind him when it happened, so I got to see the vomit up close. Some of the macaroni pieces were still whole. I think it was mac 'n' cheese, because it was all yellow—"

"Scott!" Mom shouted. "Could you please tell a different story? Perhaps one less intimately related to the inner workings of the digestive system?"

"Sorry, Mom. I'll talk about boring things. I know, how about George? He's always good for being boring."

"Your brother is not boring," said Mom.

George had been staring directly at her food. She hated thinking about gym class, even someone else's gym class. Gym class meant boys yelling at her to run faster or throw the ball harder. She would hate to run a mile on a track with a bunch of them.

"What about that play you're gonna be in with your girlfriend?" asked Scott.

"She's not my girlfriend," George said into her plate.

"Your brother didn't try out," Mom explained.

"Why not?!" Scott cried. "You spent all weekend practicing for a play about a dumb spider, and then you didn't even audition?"

"Charlotte isn't dumb!" George threw her fork down. It ricocheted off the edge of her plate and twirled end over end in the air. All eyes were on the utensil, which spun as if in slow motion. It hit the ceiling and bounced on Scott's head before rattling to the floor.

"Ow!" Scott yelled. "Did you see what he did, Mom? He tried to kill me!"

"Scott, he couldn't have done that if he tried. It was an accident and I'm sure he's sorry. Aren't you, Gee-gee?"

George nodded, in a daze. She could still feel the weight of the fork in her hands.

"Then tell your brother so," Mom said before heading to the freezer for some ice.

"Sorry, Scott," George mumbled.

Scott rubbed his head and grinned. "Man, you've got some arm on you. If you ever got in a fight, I bet you could be pretty good."

Mom returned with a plastic bag filled with several pieces of ice. Scott held the bag on his head with one hand and resumed eating with the other.

"Well," Mom said, "at least the injury hasn't affected your appetite."

The flaky fish patties and soft peas required little chewing, and soon George's plate was empty. She asked to be excused, and dumped her dishes into the stainless steel sink. She ran upstairs and closed the door to her room just as tears began to fall. She flopped onto her bed and cried into her pillow. She cried about Charlotte. She cried about being mad at Kelly. She cried about Ms. Udell thinking she was joking. But mostly, she cried about herself.

Then she pulled the denim bag from the bottom of her closet and brushed her fingers against the glossy magazines. She rubbed the cool pages against her cheeks, leaving behind tearstains that warped the covers. She told herself she didn't care whether she ruined them.

She should throw the magazines away, she thought to herself. She should get rid of them completely. But she couldn't just put them in the kitchen trash. Mom would see them and want to know where they came from. Even if George put them directly into the recycling can outside, someone might notice them. Besides, she wasn't sure whether she could dump her magazine friends like that. And even if she could, she couldn't stop wanting to be like them.

So she hugged the magazines tightly to her chest, then packed them carefully away for next time.

chapter VI

TAKEN

Mom flicked on the light in George's bedroom the next morning. "Time to get moving. My alarm never went off. You already missed the bus. I'm driving you and your brother to school."

Mom left the door of George's room ajar and cursed her way downstairs to the kitchen. George lugged her body out of bed, shrugged on some clothing, and plodded downstairs.

"Where's your backpack?" Mom asked, brushing her hair with one hand as she guided her shoes onto her feet with the other.

"Upstairs," George answered groggily.

"Well, go get it."

"What about breakfast?"

"You'll eat in the car. And don't forget your shoes!"

George gathered her things into her backpack, wiggled her feet into her sneakers, and trod back downstairs.

Mom was already by the front door, rummaging in her purse for her keys.

"Where's your brother?"

"I dunno," said George. "Probably still in bed."

"Well, go upstairs and get him. Tell him he has *one* minute to get down here, or it's no phone for a week."

"Can I pull the covers off him?"

"Sure."

George bounded up the stairs once more, this time with proper motivation. Parent-condoned sibling cruelty was a rare gift, and not to be wasted. Mom had left the light on in Scott's room, but Scott was fully asleep, snoring away. George found the two bottom corners of his thick green comforter and whisked the blanket off in one solid yank.

"Hey!" Scott grumbled.

"Mom said I could!" said George. "She also said no phone for a week if you're not downstairs in a minute."

"She just doesn't trust that I've got the situation under control," said Scott, already standing. He was wearing his favorite pair of jeans and a wrinkled black T-shirt. "I try to maximize my rest so that I can be at my best for my education, and what does she do? Complain, complain, complain." He ran his fingers through his curly hair a few times and slipped his feet into tall, unlaced boots. Then he slung his backpack over one shoulder and jogged down the stairs. George followed.

"You look like you slept in that!" Mom declared.

"I did." Scott grinned.

"And you haven't brushed your teeth, have you?"

"Nope." Scott's grin grew wider.

"You're disgusting," said Mom, resignation in her voice.

"I'm a teenage boy," said Scott. "What do you expect?"

Mom handed each of her children a granola bar, then motioned them toward the garage.

"I still don't see why I can't just take the next bus," said Scott as he buckled himself into the front passenger's seat. Scott took the city bus to high school, not a school bus like George did.

"Because the next bus isn't for forty-five minutes, and by that time you'll have missed first period." Mom backed the car out of the garage and down the driveway.

"It's only English. I already speak English real goodly."

"You're a laugh riot, Scotto." As Mom drove, she rambled on about how she needed a new alarm clock and how really her children were old enough to get up on their own anyway, and hadn't she bought Scott an alarm clock last year for Christmas for that very reason?

George stared out the backseat window, counting telephone poles. When she was little, her grandfather had told her that if she counted a hundred telephone poles in a row, an electric fairy would grant her one wish. George didn't really believe in the electric fairy anymore, and sometimes she didn't even know what she was wishing for, but counting telephone poles had become a comforting habit.

● ● ●

Room 205 buzzed as students filed in and hung their jackets and book bags in the coat closet. A group of girls gathered by the pencil sharpener around Maddy and Emma, who showed off the matching temporary pink streaks that Maddy's older sister had put into their hair the night before.

Ms. Udell subtly pointed at George and motioned with one finger for her to come up to the teacher's desk. The desk had probably been in the same room since the school was built; it might have been even older than Ms. Udell. The original shiny coating was worn away completely in some places and deeply scratched in the rest. If you dug your fingernail into the desk hard enough, you could leave a mark in the waxy varnish.

"You surprised me yesterday, George," Ms. Udell said, her reading glasses perched on her head. "I can't cast you as Charlotte, of course. I have too many girls who want the part."

"I know." George hoped that Ms. Udell would let her take her seat.

"But," Ms. Udell continued, "you did a good job. You have passion and dedication. Are you sure you don't want another part? You could be Wilbur."

Wilbur, the dirty pig. George shook her head. That would be worse than not being in the play at all.

"Or one of the other boys' parts. Templeton? Mr. Zuckerman? The gander?"

"No, thanks."

"Perhaps a narrator, then? The narrators have a really important role. They keep the audience informed."

George shook her head. She didn't want to be in the play, watching someone else be Charlotte.

"Well, okay." Ms. Udell eyed George warily. "I guess you can be in the crew."

The classroom door opened and Kelly bounded in. "Did I get a part? Did I?"

Ms. Udell's focus turned to the bubble of ebullience bouncing in front of her. "Kelly, you will find out about your part when everyone else does. At the end of the day."

Kelly gave an exaggerated sigh and headed off to the coat closet to join the group of girls huddled around Maddy and Emma. Ms. Udell turned back to where George had been, but George had already disappeared to her seat.

As promised, Ms. Udell didn't share the names of the students in the play until the final moments of the school day, at which point she distributed scripts to the actors and gave some advice on how to memorize their lines.

Kelly would be Charlotte. When she found out, she jumped nearly out of her seat and whooped with glee. Then she turned to smile at George, but George had turned her head to face the closet, shielding her eyes from view with her hand. It was bad enough that she wouldn't be Charlotte. Now she would have to listen to Kelly talk about it, and possibly nothing else, for the next three weeks.

Ms. Udell continued to read the cast list. Chris would play Templeton. He let out a deep "yeeeeah" and pumped his fist in the air. Maddy, Emma, and several other kids would play the barnyard animals, and most of the rest of the kids who had tried out would be nar-rators. Kids from Mr. Jackson's class would be playing the parts of Wilbur and Fern. George's name wasn't said at all.

George knew she couldn't have possibly expected to hear Ms. Udell call her name. Still, her heart sank. She had genuinely started to believe that if people could see her onstage as Charlotte, maybe they would see that she was a girl offstage too.

When her row was called, George grabbed her book bag and got away from the other kids at the closet as quickly as she could. She packed her math workbook and her science reader.

Room 205 headed down to the yard for dismissal. George didn't pay attention when the class stopped to regroup. Several times, she bumped into the backpack in front of her.

The moment the class stepped onto the school yard, Kelly dashed out of the girls' line and over to George.

"How come you're not in the play?" she asked. "Ms. Udell said everyone who tried out would get a part. And I thought for sure Ms. Udell would make you Wilbur. You were so good this weekend. Rehearsals are going to be totally boring without you."

Another voice chimed in: "Yeah, George, how come you're not in the play?"

George cringed, recognizing Rick's voice behind him. Jeff almost never talked directly to George unless he had something really mean to say, but George wasn't surprised to see them both there when she turned around.

"Last week, you were all crying about the poor little spider," Rick continued. "And we saw you go out and audition. How bad did you have to be for Chris to get the part?"

"I'll bet he read the stupid spider's part by mistake!" Jeff smirked. "He's such a freaking girl anyway."

Jeff guffawed, and Rick laughed alongside him.

"Don't listen to them." Kelly tugged at the elbow of her best friend's shirt, but George stood, stuck in place. The hairs on her arms stood straight up, and the back of her neck tingled.

"Or maybe he just read it all backward," said Rick.

"Knio! Knio!" Jeff made a horrific sound, attempting to oink backward. Rick joined him, and they snorted across the playground toward the gate, where parents sat in cars in a line down the block.

She didn't exhale until Rick and Jeff passed through the gate. They didn't know her secret, or else they wouldn't have dropped it so quickly, but their guess had been so close that George's cheeks flushed with shame. She relaxed her hands, which had formed into fists, but her teeth were still clenched.

"They're jerks," said Kelly. "You're not a girl."

"What if I am?" George was startled by her own words.

Kelly drew back in surprise. "What? That's ridiculous. You're a boy. I mean"—she pointed vaguely downward at George—"you have a *you-know-what*, right?"

"Yeah, but . . ." George trailed off and looked at the ground. She kicked a small rock that skipped into a tuft of grass. She didn't feel like a boy.

They stood together in a heavy silence. Kelly's brow furrowed in thought. After a few moments, she spoke. "You know, I thought about whether I was a boy once. Back when I wanted to be a firefighter and I thought all firefighters were boys. Is it like that?"

"I don't think so, Kelly."

The lines in front of the buses had mostly disappeared and the drivers were only waiting for the final okay to start their routes. They had begun to turn over their engines, and the air filled with heavy rumbling and the fumes of diesel exhaust.

George had a sudden frightening thought and

grabbed Kelly's arm just above the elbow. "Don't tell anyone."

"I won't."

George's grip on Kelly's arm grew uncomfortable. "Not even your dad."

"Not even my dad."

They ran to their respective buses, the soles of their sneakers slapping on the blacktop, calling "One-two-three!" and "Zoot!" behind them.

● ● ●

The school bus left George at the corner and drove off, its engine straining to pick up speed. George walked the half block to her house and turned up the driveway. She fumbled with the house key, balancing her book bag on one knee while she turned the key to the right, but the door was already unlocked, and pushed open easily. Mom sat on the couch.

"You're home!" said George.

"What's this about?" asked Mom. Her expression was flat. George's denim bag swung slowly in the air, hanging from one crooked finger. The zipper was open.

George's heart pounded, and for a moment, she thought she might burst on the spot. She took a deep gulp of air.

"I was feeling under the weather today, so I came back home to do some cleaning," said Mom. "Your closet was a mess . . . and I found these. Did you steal them?"

"No!" George's face was hot. "I . . . I collected them."

"Don't lie to me. Where did you get them?" Mom pulled out the copy of *Seventeen* from last October, the smiling twins on the cover unaware of Mom's tight grip.

"I found them in different places."

Mom eyed George, her eyebrows thick and heavy. She stood, with a deep sigh.

"George, I don't want to find you wearing my clothes. Or my shoes. That kind of thing was cute when you were three. You're not three anymore. In fact, I don't want to see you in my room at all."

"But I didn't . . . ," George began, but Mom ignored her.

Mom disappeared to her bedroom with the denim bag in her hand. George remained by the front door, her mouth slightly open.

She couldn't believe her friends were gone.

chapter VII

TIME DRAGS
WHEN YOU'RE MISERABLE

The days passed George by in a haze of unhappiness. She dragged herself through her daily routine. She dragged herself out of bed in the morning and to the bathroom. She dragged herself downstairs and dragged her spoon through her cereal and up to her mouth. She dragged herself to the bus stop, through the day, and back home again.

Kelly didn't call once that week, and George didn't call her. They didn't even eat lunch together. Kelly ate with the other lead actors and talked about the play. When Kelly did look George's way, she gave George an awkward, forced smile. George ate lunch by herself that week.

On Thursday, she sat down without looking, and realized she was directly across from Jeff and Rick. She spent the entire lunch period staring at her lunch tray and listening to them snicker about Mrs. Fields, the kindergartners, and, of course, George.

At home, Mom didn't say anything about George's bag, or much of anything else, either. She went about her day with a stony face and rigid movements. George tried to avoid being in the same room with her. She ate her dinner as quickly as she could, skipped all but her favorite shows on TV, and spent as much time in her room as possible. And she couldn't stop thinking about her magazines.

Saturday morning, when there was a heavy *knock knock* on her bedroom door, George expected Mom. Instead, she was surprised to see her brother holding up two video game driving wheels. "Wanna play *Mario Kart*?"

Scott hadn't asked George to play video games in months. They used to play almost every day. George would come home after school to find Scott on the couch, watching wrestling and ignoring his homework. They would play until Mom got home and yelled at them to turn off the TV and get their homework done. Now Scott usually came home just in time for dinner, if not later.

"Why?" George asked, still deep in her fog of misery.

"If Mom catches me on the couch playing video games, she'll make me do chores. But if I'm playing a game with my *kid brother*"—Scott ruffled George's already messy hair—"she'll call it fraternal bonding or something, and maybe let us play a few more rounds."

Scott's reason seemed selfish enough to be genuine, so George joined Scott in the living room and took a seat on the right side of the couch. They selected their cars and drivers. Scott drove as Bowser, the reptilian archvillain of the Nintendo game series. He loved being able to knock into the smaller characters and send them flying. George selected Toad. She liked the happy sounds the little mushroom made. When she was alone, she sometimes drove as the princess, but she didn't dare choose her in front of Scott.

A creature in the sky floated down with a checkered flag in its hands. After a brief countdown, the race was on. The pack of characters vied for the lead, throwing obstacles and running through one another while invincible. Scott and George made their way through the maze.

At the announcement of the final lap, they were in first and second place. The computer players were nearly half a lap behind. As they turned into the last long straightaway, George shot a red shell into the void ahead of her. The shell whooped along until it slammed into Scott, sending him spiraling in the air. On-screen, Bowser pumped his fist in anger and slowly puttered back onto the road. He was a heavy beast, and took a long time to gain speed. Toad zipped past and into the lead. The finish line was just ahead, and George crossed it moments before Scott caught up.

Scott roared like a dinosaur and shook his wheel in the air. George giggled.

"You know," Scott said, "that's the first time I've heard you laugh in about a week."

"Yeah," George said.

"Girl problems?" Scott asked, his eyes focused on the television screen as the cloud creature announced the start of the next course.

"No," George said. She knew that wasn't true. Being a secret girl was a giant problem.

"What about Kelly?"

"I've told you," George said through gritted teeth, "she is *not* my girlfriend." She bit her lip as she veered around a sharp corner.

"I haven't seen you on the phone with her all week."

"Just forget it."

"Are you two having a fight?"

"NO!" The wheel felt moist in George's clammy palms.

Scott laughed before knocking a car into a pool of lava.

"What's so funny?"

"Sure sounds like you're having a fight."

"Shut up, Scott."

"Whatever. She's not *my* girlfriend."

"SHUT UP!!" George turned to her brother, turning the wheel along with her. Toad screamed his way down a ravine as the lower half of the screen fell into a deep, dark hole. "See what you made me do?"

Scott pulled into the lead for the final lap. George climbed into fifth place by the time she crossed the finish line, but it still put her third in the overall rankings.

They played the third round in deadly silence, racing through the final lap as competitively as if they were in the Indianapolis 500. They were battling for first and second place when Mario came through. He shimmered with invincibility and ran through both Scott's and George's cars, sending them flying into the air and falling back down to the track at a dead stop. They hobbled over the finish line, booed at the defeated music that played on the television, and vowed together to crush Mario in the fourth and final round of the match.

Scott bumped into Mario with his massive force, and George used her speed mushrooms to plow through him at top speed. They laughed their way across the final line. They came in fourth and sixth places, delighted that Mario had ended dead last.

Scott and George played another game of *Mario Kart*, and another, until Scott insisted on switching to a shooter game. He promised George that it was fun and that she would enjoy it. She didn't, and after a few minutes, she left Scott to kill everything in sight.

chapter VIII

SOME JERK

The school yard filled with kids on Monday morning. Younger boys played kick the rock and ran about wildly, while older boys crowded around electronic gadgets that were hidden in the bottoms of backpacks during the school day. George leaned against the chain-link fence, watching some girls from her class jump rope. She knew the rhymes they sang, but no one would ask her to join. Boys didn't play jump rope.

"Hi," a small voice spoke behind George. It was Kelly. She wore a faded blue shirt with a smiling whale on it that read I'M HAVING A WHALE OF A TIME.

"I'm sorry I got the part of Charlotte." She twisted the toe of her sneaker into the blacktop pavement.

George shrugged.

"Are you mad at me?" Kelly asked.

"No."

"Good."

Kelly took a deep breath. "And I'm sorry I ignored you last week." She scratched her neck. "And you know what? If you think you're a girl . . ."

George braced for Kelly's next words.

"Then I think you're a girl too!" Kelly leaped onto her best friend and gave her a hug so big they both nearly toppled over. The openmouthed surprise and joy on George's face only made Kelly smile harder.

"So you're, like, transgender or something?" Kelly whispered as best she could in her excitement. "I was reading on the Internet, and there are lots of people like you. Did you know you can take hormones so that your body, you know, doesn't go all manlike?"

"Yeah, I know." George had been reading websites about transitioning since Scott had taught her how to clear the web browser history on Mom's computer. "But you need your parents' permission."

"Your mom's pretty cool," Kelly said, her eyebrows lifted. "Maybe she'd be okay with it."

George shook her head and looked down, staring at her shoelaces. Even without closing her eyes, she could see her denim bag hanging from Mom's long finger, swinging slightly. The words *It's not cute anymore* echoed in her mind. She told Kelly about her bag of girls' magazines, and about Mom taking it.

"But that's not fair!" Kelly was indignant. "You didn't steal them! What right does she have to take them from you?"

"Sometimes *transgender* people don't get rights." George had read on the Internet about transgender people being treated unfairly.

"That's awful."

"I know."

After an awkward silence, Kelly showed George some pictures she'd taken that weekend at the park. Many of them were close-ups of leaves, and some of them were quite striking. The ways the light hit different parts of the leaves made them look three-dimensional.

Kelly drew her camera out of her pocket. Then she started giving out directions as she circled around George, shooting away. "Smile more, like you just got a present. Now surprise, when you open the gift. And joy, like you just got what you always wanted."

George frowned. "Could you take pictures of the face I'm making, instead of telling me what face I should have?"

"I'm just trying to provide a little artistic direction. Never mind." She put her camera back in her pocket and joined a group of girls playing hopscotch. George leaned against the fence and looked up at the cloudy sky.

When the bell rang, the playground formed into girls' and boys' lines for each class. Once upstairs, George settled into her seat and began the assignment written on the board. It asked her to find as many words as possible that she could create from the letters of the word *PERFORMANCE*. George stared at the three words on her page: *PERFORM, MORE,* and *FOR.* She refused to write down *MAN*, even though it kept smacking her in the face, blocking her view of other words. George still had the same three words on her page when Ms. Udell began her morning announcements.

"As you are aware, our play is fast approaching. It's time for us to kick into high gear. We will be limiting our traditional academic endeavors to the forenoon hours." Ms. Udell ignored the blank stares she received from the class. "The time after you ingest your midday nourishment will be entirely devoted to theatrical pursuits."

"I think she means no work after lunch!" Chris called out.

"I most certainly do not!" Ms. Udell held a stern look for a moment before breaking into a grin. "But I do mean that we will be in the classroom only until lunch-time. The auditorium echoes, and I want the cast to get some experience projecting their voices properly. Plus, the crew needs to put together our set."

The class cheered—some for the play, but most because they would have less classwork. Kelly cheered loudest of all, but George remained silent. She didn't want to go into *high gear*. She didn't want to think about Charlotte anymore. She wanted the play to be over and done with. The only good part of Ms. Udell's plan was that it meant the class would skip afternoon gym.

Ms. Udell quieted the students and continued. "That does *not* mean that we won't be working hard in the mornings. In fact, we'll need to be twice as efficient. And I'm sure I don't need to remind you"—Ms. Udell eyed Jeff, Rick, and then Kelly—"that students who cannot keep their attention on their studies in the morning will be sent to another classroom in the afternoon to complete them, as well as additional written assignments."

The morning passed in a drone of vocabulary, fractions, and reading. Not another word about the play was said until lunch, when the long lunchroom table burst into a flurry of excitement. Kelly said she knew all about voice projection, and she would be happy to help anyone who needed some coaching. No one took her up on it.

When the bell to end recess rang, Ms. Udell met her class in the playground instead of waiting for them upstairs as she usually did. Mr. Jackson stood beside her. Ms. Udell took the cast to the auditorium to practice onstage, leaving the remainder of the fourth grade in the school yard with Mr. Jackson to form the crew.

Mr. Jackson was a tall black man with a mostly bald head and a thick mustache. He called his crew to sit in a circle under the rusted basketball hoop. A half-dozen cans of paint, a bag of brushes, some buckets, a heap of cardboard, and several large tarps waited in a pile underneath the bent rim.

"Okay. We've hashed out costumes, props, and music," said Mr. Jackson. "Now it's time to create the backdrop for our actors, to bring literature to life! Remember, the lifeblood of a play is its crew. If the actors are like Wilbur, the star of the fair, then we are like Charlotte, the unseen heroes who got him there. Now let's help our stars put on *SOME PERFORMANCE*."

Before the crew could begin painting, Mr. Jackson said they needed to develop a game plan. They argued about where to sketch hay bales, the pig trough, and Templeton's nest, and whether they needed to paint the Arables' kitchen at all. But everyone agreed that a dark corner at the top right would be perfect for Charlotte and her webs. Mr. Jackson would provide a ladder to set up behind the backdrop for Charlotte to appear from above.

George kept quiet until it was time to choose members of the crew to help out onstage, but then her hand was up first. If she couldn't be Charlotte, she could at least deliver the large cards with the painted spiderweb words on them to Kelly. She would also hold the ladder steady while Kelly performed from the top. She would be Charlotte's Charlotte, deeply hidden in the shadows.

Two girls and a boy from Mr. Jackson's class would carry props onstage and off. Rick volunteered to raise the curtain. Jeff didn't sign up for a job. He said he'd rather eat a spider than come back to school in the evening. The stagehands were advised to wear all black on the day of the performances so they wouldn't stand out during the show.

Finally, it was time to get to work painting the main backdrop for the play. The crew laid heavy tarps over the cracked blacktop yard. The tarps were covered in blobs and trails of yellow, blue, orange, and red. The canvas stuck to itself and crackled as the students unfolded it. Mr. Jackson handed out smocks made from large men's button-down shirts. Jeff refused to wear one, saying it looked too much like a dress. Four students unfolded a mass of white cloth to lay out over the tarp. It was made from two flat bedsheets sewn together, and would be their backdrop.

Each member of the crew was given an assignment. George's job was to paint the pig trough. She laid down a base of brown paint. Once the edges dried a bit, she would outline it and add some detail in black. While she was waiting, she dunked her brush into a plastic cup of mucky, murky water. She swished the paintbrush around, watching the brown sludge swirl, revealing wisps of green. As she was sweeping the paintbrush across a corner of canvas to dry out the brush, she heard Jeff and Rick chatting.

"What do you wanna pull the curtain for?" said Jeff, his voice filled with disdain.

"I don't know," said Rick. "I just, you know, thought it would be fun."

"I think it would be more fun to pull the curtain down right in the middle of the show!" Jeff laughed.

Rick gave a hollow chuckle. "Yeah, sure."

"Oh, come on, Rick! What's your deal? All of a sudden, it's like you care about this dumb play. Look at you, worried about how many strings there are on a thing of hay."

"They're called bales, and Mr. Jackson said that the string is called twine."

"Who cares?" said Jeff. "You're being a suck-up."

"I am not!" Rick yelled, and flicked his brush at Jeff. A stream of yellow sun streaked down the white cotton sheet. "Now look what you made me do." Rick searched for a rag and tried to wipe off the paint.

"Whatever." Even though George couldn't see him, she knew Jeff was rolling his eyes.

"What's the big deal anyway? She's just a stupid spider. Do you know what I'd do if I met a talking spider?" Jeff waited for Rick to respond, but Rick was focused on his brushstrokes. Jeff's wide brush sat in a pool of yellow on the tarp below a half-painted hay bale.

"I'd step on her. Crush her under my foot like the freak she is. Freaky spider. Stupid, freaky spider." Jeff began to sing an unformed tune. *"Stupid, freaky spider. I'm gonna step on you because it's what you deserve, you stupid, freaky spi-i-der. I'm glad you diiiiiiiieeed."*

George's face felt hot. Jeff had no right to talk about Charlotte like that. Jeff was always saying something mean. Charlotte wouldn't stand for it, and George wouldn't either.

She grabbed a blank piece of paper, a cup of black paint, and a thin brush. She laid out the paper and set to work. By the time she was done, she was quite pleased with her own creation. Charlotte wasn't the only one who could express herself through the well-crafted word.

George lifted the paper carefully and held it at her side between a finger and her thumb. She was so worried about whether the paint was already dry or whether the paper would smear against her leg that she barely thought about what she was doing or who she was doing it to. Meanwhile, her feet propelled her fast and hard toward her target.

Jeff was lying facedown on the pavement. He slathered a blue sky on the top of the canvas, leaving gobs of paint as he worked. Rick crouched nearby, painting a black line around the edge of a hay bale.

As George passed Jeff, she dropped the paper. It was a direct hit, landing perfectly on his back, right in the middle of his white T-shirt.

"Hey, what the heck?" Jeff's head whipped around.

"Sorry," said George. She whisked the paper off his back and grinned wildly.

"What a klutz," Jeff snorted, and returned to his blue sky. He had no idea that the words SOME JERK glistened in black paint on his shirt, fashioned inside a simple spiderweb. Jeff was SOME JERK, and now everyone would know it.

George bit her tongue to keep from laughing out loud. It had worked! The *J* was backward, but the words were clear. George crumpled up the paper and threw it into the big black trash bag.

It wasn't until George sat back down that she froze. The color drained from her face, and her tongue seemed to swell. Jeff would realize what had happened soon, and he would know who had done it. She was dead. D-E-A-D. Dead.

George eyed Jeff nervously until Mr. Jackson announced it was time to pack up. Without cleaning a thing, Jeff lined up along the fence, and Rick followed. Suddenly, there was a gasp from Rick, and a scream from Jeff. Jeff whipped his T-shirt around.

"What the . . . ?" His voice trailed off as he met Mr. Jackson's glare, but his eyes gleamed with fury. He rubbed his shirt as best he could, but it was too late; the paint was dry. Jeff gave up and turned it inside out, the tag pointing up and into his hair.

George could smell her own sweat. Her neck felt hot, then cold and wet, then hot again. Her body wanted to run. Then Jeff was right in front of her. Rick was behind her.

"Hey, Rick. It looks like someone's finally starting to grow some balls." Jeff thumped his right fist into his left palm.

George looked down at her feet and hoped that neither of the boys noticed the flush that filled her cheeks. There was nothing George dreaded more than when boys talked about what was in her underpants. Her cheeks grew so hot that she felt like metal. She wished she *were* made of metal, with laser eyes that could slice Jeff in two.

But she wasn't made of metal, and her eyes were as helpless as the rest of her. Jeff was a head taller, and he was thick too. Jeff's pinkie was the size of George's index finger, and Jeff kept pounding his fist into his other hand. Rick stood behind George. He wasn't as tall as Jeff, but he was taller than George, and stronger.

Putting a hand on each of her shoulders, Rick easily held her in place. George felt a hard pit forming deep in her stomach. She looked over at Mr. Jackson, who was surrounded by students and art supplies.

"You think you're funny, don't you, freak? You think you can mess with me? You're such a freak. You're a freak. Freak. Freak." Jeff flicked his finger against George's forehead with each *freak*. His words crawled under her skin, settling deep into the crevices of her bones.

Without warning, Jeff pumped his arm back and launched his fist into George's stomach. She stumbled a few steps back into the chain fence, doubled over, and clutched at her waist, gasping for breath.

George's body spasmed. She retched once. She retched twice. She opened her mouth wide and vomit spewed forth in an arc that started at Jeff's shoes and splattered all the way up to his face. Then she slumped to the ground in a heap.

"Ew!" Jeff screamed, wiping his face and then looking at his hands in horror. "Ewwwww!!!"

Rick snickered.

"Shut up!" yelled Jeff, tearing off the shirt he was already wearing inside out because of the web declaring him SOME JERK. He wiped his face and spit furiously. He reeked of the acidic barf that dripped down his pants. Chunks of burger and corn soaked his shoes. He jumped away in horror, but couldn't get away from the stench.

Mr. Jackson ran over to the scene. "Now, what's going on here?" he asked. "George, are you okay?"

Jeff was a sputtering, shirtless mess. George was still

on the ground, holding her stomach, tears in her eyes. A crowd of students had gathered around.

"That kid punched that other kid," said a boy from Mr. Jackson's class, pointing at Jeff. "And then *that* kid"—his finger turned to George—"went BLECCCCCH and hurled and it flew and landed all over that kid." His finger pointed back at Jeff.

"Thank you very much for the play-by-play, Isaiah. Now if you would please get in line." Mr. Jackson addressed the fourth graders. "In fact, if you would all please get in line. Jeff, I want you at the very front with me. George, you too."

Mr. Jackson helped George up. George's stomach hurt, and her mouth felt raw. The word *freak* echoed between her ears. She followed Mr. Jackson and Jeff, who was still shirtless, into the school. The outside world felt distant, and she couldn't make out the whispers of the fourth graders behind her.

On the way, Mr. Jackson stopped at the main office to get a school T-shirt for Jeff. Ms. Davis, the school secretary, brought one out. She had a small face, an even smaller nose, and short dark hair that grayed at the temples.

"This vomit reeks," Jeff complained. "I gotta clean up first."

Ms. Davis sighed. "I'll take them, Mr. Jackson." She turned to Jeff and George. "But I'm coming in with you. No monkey business."

George, Jeff, and Ms. Davis went into the boys' bathroom together. George hovered by the trash can near the door.

"Don't you want to wash up too?" the secretary asked.

George shook her head. Her mouth still tasted of sick.

"Suit yourself."

Jeff put his head under the faucet to rinse it, and wadded up a bunch of paper towels to wipe down his upper body. He put his shirt in the sink and ran water on it, but Ms. Davis told him to hurry up. Jeff grumbled, wrung out his shirt, and put on the T-shirt she had given him.

Ms. Davis walked Jeff and George back to Room 205. Ms. Udell and Ms. Davis whispered at the door for a few moments. Then Ms. Davis stepped inside the classroom, and Ms. Udell came out into the hallway.

"Mr. Jackson spoke with me about the incident in the yard," she said in her iciest voice. "Jeffrey, can you please explain to me why you punched George in the stomach?"

"He ruined my shirt!" Jeff shouted.

"*Mr. Forrester.*" Ms. Udell addressed Jeff by his last name. "I will thank you not to yell in the hallway. Further, there is no excuse for violence on school grounds, or anywhere else, for that matter. Much less for the sake of a shirt. Mr. Jackson is writing up an incident report. When he is done, Ms. Davis will escort you both back down to the main office, where your parents have been called and will be picking you up."

George and Jeff waited in the hallway with Ms. Davis, Jeff shooting evil looks George's way the whole time. George stared at the ground. Once the incident report was done, the three of them headed down to the main office. George sat on the bench by the teachers' old-time clock, her feet dangling below her. Jeff sat in a folding chair next to Ms. Davis, facing the window, kicking the desk until Ms. Davis told him to quit it. He would stop for about a minute, and then resume kicking, softly at first, until Ms. Davis yelled at him again.

George's mom entered the office and rushed past George without even noticing her. Ms. Davis pointed her directly into Principal Maldonado's office and advised George to follow.

George had never been in the principal's office before and was surprised by how bright it was. Orange curtains framed windows that reached nearly to the ceiling, and piles of books were stacked around the room. Principal Maldonado sat at a large desk in the center of the room and invited Mom and George to sit across from her in two brown cushioned chairs. The principal had short gray hair and wore a turquoise necklace over a black turtleneck. She was a fat woman whose broad shoulders filled her chair with an easy self-confidence.

"Now, Mrs. Mitchell, George has defaced student property, and that is a serious offense. However, given the nature of the incident, as well as lack of a prior record on George's part, I would just as soon resolve this as simply as possible."

As the principal spoke, George's eyes scanned the wall behind her. List upon list of phone numbers and email addresses were taped up to the lower half, interspersed with handwritten notes held up with thumbtacks pressed directly into the wall. Dozens of signs hung above, telling kids to eat right, not to take drugs, to do their homework, and not to be a bully. A sign in the far corner showed a large rainbow flag flying on a black background. Below the flag, the sign said SUPPORT SAFE SPACES FOR GAY, LESBIAN, BISEXUAL, AND TRANSGENDER YOUTH.

Reading the word *transgender* sent a shiver down George's spine. She wondered where she could find a safe space like that, and if there would be other girls like her there. Maybe they could talk about makeup together. Maybe they could even try some on.

George stared at the sign and thought about finding other girls like her while Mom and the principal chatted. Principal Maldonado asked about recent changes in home life—but there hadn't been any since Dad left three years ago. Finally, the principal said, "Why don't you take George home for the day to give him some time to cool down, and we'll leave it at that."

Mom thanked Principal Maldonado, who then turned her attention to George. "I wouldn't make a habit of bothering Jeff. Some kids like trouble, and they'll do whatever they can to find it. And if you land back in this office again, I can promise you I won't be so lenient."

George hoped she'd never find out what that meant.

chapter IX

DINNER AT ARNIE'S

Mom didn't say anything in the car about the fight. Instead, she turned on a radio station that promised *v-v-v-vintage modern rock* and sang along with the choruses. When they got home, Mom suggested George wash up.

In the bathroom, George combed her hair forward. If she squinted at the mirror, she almost looked like a girl. For now, anyway. Today her skin was smooth, but someday testosterone would grow a terrible beard all over her face. Scott had already started to sprout awkward tufts under his chin.

She brushed her hair back to its usual style and headed to her room to flop on her bed. A few minutes later, a quiet knock came on her bedroom door.

"Can I come in?" Mom asked.

"Yeah." George sat up and Mom took a seat at the foot of the bed.

"George, I'm going to be honest. I worry about you. There are a lot of kids like Jeff out there, and plenty who are worse." Mom blew a puff of air up at her bangs. "I mean, being gay is one thing. Kids are coming out much earlier than when I was young. It won't be easy, but we'll deal with it. But being *that* kind of gay?" Mom shook her head. "That's something else entirely."

"I'm not any kind of gay." At least, George didn't think she was gay. She didn't know who she liked, really, boys or girls.

"Then why did I find all those girls' magazines in your closet?" Mom raised an eyebrow, and a curved wrinkle formed across her forehead.

George drew in a deep breath, held it, and let it out. Then another.

"Because I'm a girl."

Mom's face relaxed and she gave a short laugh. "Is that what this is about? Oh, Gee, I was there when you were born. I changed your diapers, and I promise you, you are one hundred percent boy. Besides, you're only ten years old. You don't know how you'll feel in a few years."

George's heart sank. She couldn't wait years. She could hardly wait another minute.

"Tell you what," Mom said, patting George's knee. "How about we do something special tonight. Let's go to Arnie's." Arnie's All-You-Can-Eat Buffet was George's favorite restaurant. "You'll feel better once you're eating nachos and pizza and pie like a regular kid. For now, just chill for a bit. That's what I'm going to do."

George knew Mom was trying to make her feel better, but it didn't work. Nothing—certainly not a buffet dinner—could help the fact that Mom didn't see her.

Mom took her laptop into her bedroom and came out only to refill her seltzer glass. Once again, George wished she had her magazines to look at. Instead, she watched cartoons on the sofa until school was over at three. She knew it took Kelly about twenty minutes to get home on the bus—and sure enough, the house phone rang at 3:22. George picked up the cordless extension and headed to her room.

"What happened to you?" Kelly asked, not bothering to say hello. "Everyone's saying you picked a fight with Jeff. But I told them that was impossible because you've never been in a fight in your life, and that Jeff must have been the one to start it. I mean, really, who's gonna pick a fight—you or Jeff? What did he do to you? Are you okay? I mean, you're obviously not in the hospital or anything, but man, they said he got you good. And did you really throw up on him? Because seriously, that might be the funniest thing I've ever heard in my life."

Kelly was so loud that George could feel the phone vibrate. She held it a few inches from her ear and waited until Kelly was done.

"Are you there?" Kelly asked.

"Yeah."

"Yeah, what? Yeah, you're there? Yeah, you threw up on Jeff? Or yeah, you picked a fight?"

"All three."

"What the heck, George? What were you doing, picking a fight with the biggest bully in our class?"

"I dunno. He made fun of Charlotte, I guess." George's reasoning sounded foolish, even to her.

"Charlotte's not even real."

"Yeah, but—"

"If you're gonna be transgender and all, you're going to have to be a lot more careful. You won't be able to throw up on every bully you meet."

"I could try," said George. "Bleh! Bleh! Bleh!"

"You sound like a vomiting machine gun."

"I could be a superhero!"

"You'd be Ralph the Ralpher. You could even have a motto: 'If you throw down, I'll throw up!'"

George and Kelly chuckled, but then a quiet fell over the conversation, and the only sound that came through the phone was the airy hum of the line itself.

"The play really means a lot to you, doesn't it?" asked Kelly, breaking the silence.

"It's just . . ." George sighed. "I just thought that . . . you know . . . if I were Charlotte in the play, my mom might . . ."

"See that you're a girl?"

"Yeah," said George. It felt funny to hear Kelly call her a girl—but in a good way, like a tickling in her stomach that reminded her she was real.

"Well, maybe it's not too late," said Kelly. "I mean, the play hasn't happened yet, has it?"

"But you got the part."

"There are two performances, silly. I could take one and you could have the other."

"You'd do that for me?"

"Of course I would. I thought about it the whole bus ride home. I can make sure my dad comes to the afternoon show. You could totally do it! In fact, you make a better Charlotte than I do."

It was true. George had listened to Charlotte's lines enough times that she knew every word, and she knew just how she would say them—mostly like Kelly did, but different in a few key places. Kelly emphasized some of the wrong words, and she still sometimes flubbed Charlotte's first line by saying "SalutaTAtions" instead of "Salutations."

"But how?"

"It's easier than easy! You'll already be dressed in black as a stagehand. All you have to do is put on the arm vest and you'll look perfect." As Charlotte, Kelly wore a black leotard and tights, along with a vest with three stuffed arms sewn on either side.

"But Ms. Udell already said I couldn't have the part."

"You know what? Ms. Udell is wrong. You should be Charlotte. And by the time she realizes it's you, it'll be too late. You'll already be onstage and there won't be a thing she can do about it."

George could practically hear the devious grin on Kelly's face, and she could certainly feel the grin on hers. With Kelly's help, maybe she really could be Charlotte.

"But what about when the other kids notice?"

"Forget the other kids. Jeff won't be there, and no one else will care."

"What about my mom?"

"I thought showing your mom was part of the idea!" Kelly's shrieking voice hurtled through the phone.

"Yeah, but . . ." George's stomach flopped.

"Look, do you want your mom to know you're a girl?"

"Yes."

"Then be Charlotte." Kelly said it as if it was choosing strawberry ice cream instead of chocolate. "I gotta go. I still have one performance to rehearse for. And now, so do you! One-two-three—"

"ZOOT!" George hung up and twirled around the house, like Charlotte spinning a glorious spiderweb. She, George, was going to be Charlotte onstage! In front of Mom and everyone!

The butterflies in her stomach had butterflies in *their* stomachs.

● ● ●

Scott leaped out of Randy's house the moment Mom honked the horn, as though he had been waiting at the doorknob. He filled the car with a rant about his history teacher, followed by a tirade about his math teacher and a torrent about his biology teacher.

"The man wants us to dissect a worm!"

"I would think you would find that gruesomeness appealing," said Mom.

"Not if I have to diagram every last body part to scale. It's going to be a pain in the butt. If I'm going to diagram something, why can't it at least be a frog? That would be cool."

"If you think it's hard on you, just imagine how the worm feels."

George was glad that Scott was diverting Mom's attention. She didn't want to be asked why she was smiling after having been beaten up and sent home from school, but she was ecstatic about the idea of playing Charlotte onstage, and it was hard not to show it.

Mom turned in to Arnie's All-You-Can-Eat Buffet and rolled into a spot facing the building. Red awnings with thick green borders hung across the wide windows of the large, squat building. A long banner stretching across the front of the restaurant proclaimed OVER ONE HUNDRED ITEMS COOKED FRESH EVERY DAY.

Inside, happy eaters sat at booths and tables, their plates filled with food foraged from a dozen different cuisines in heaps of each person's favorites. No one waited on tables at Arnie's, and no one waited for their meals. Instead, endless buffet trays lined one long wall of the restaurant. People dressed all in white carried out full trays of food to the buffet and brought empty trays back into the kitchen. Tables filled with soda and lemonade glasses.

Mom paid at the door and unleashed her children on the buffet while she found a table. George filled her plate with fried chicken, mashed potatoes, corn fritters, pizza, a pile of nachos, and a cube of cherry Jell-O hidden under a taco, to eat while Mom was getting her own food. Even at Arnie's, Mom said you should have dinner before dessert. George went back to the table while Mom took her turn at the buffet. Scott sat down soon after.

"What's up with Mom?" he asked from behind

a plate piled high with ham, turkey, and chicken, topped with two slices of pizza. "She never takes us out to Arnie's on a weekday unless she's upset about something."

"Yeah, well." George looked over at Mom, who was still picking out lettuce for her salad. "I kind of got into a fight at school."

Scott's head shot up in surprise and his brow grew heavy. "When I got into a fight at school, I got grounded. How did you work Arnie's out of it?"

"I kind of also told her something."

"It must have been big. Mom's staring at the beets like a zombie."

"It was."

"Did you tell her you were gay?" Scott twisted his fork into a pile of mashed potatoes. "You know I'm okay with that, right? Before Dad left, he made me promise to take care of you. He said you were like that."

"I'm not gay," George said. Why did everyone think she was gay?

"Whatever. I don't care. My friend Matt is gay. It's no big deal."

But it was a big deal. "I told her I think I'm a girl."

"Oh." That was all Scott said at first. "Oh."

Scott chewed, swallowed, and took another bite of pizza. The background noise of the restaurant throbbed in George's ears. She wished Scott would say something, even if it was mean.

"Ohhh." Scott took a bite of turkey. "Ohhhhhhhhh." Scott began to nod slowly. He turned to George, whose stomach had jumped with each *oh* and was now nearly in her throat.

"That's more than just being gay. No wonder she's freaking out."

"I know."

Scott put down his fork. "So do you?"

"Do I what?"

"Think you're a girl?"

"Yes." George was surprised at how easy that question was to answer.

"Oh." Scott ripped a hunk off a roll with his teeth and chewed thoughtfully.

Mom returned with a green salad, topped with raw vegetables and vinaigrette dressing. She finished it quickly and dropped her plate off in a dish bin. Mom always started her meal at Arnie's with a salad. She said it was healthy, not to mention delicious, but she always ate it quickly and then returned with a plate just as decadent as George's and Scott's.

Scott had gnawed silently on a chicken wing while Mom ate her salad, but once she got up and approached the appetizer bar, he dropped the bone onto his plate.

"I know about your magazines," he said.

"Mom *told* you?"

"Naw, I found them this weekend. I knew Mom was upset about something, and then I saw the bag sitting on her bed. Dude, I thought you had porn or something in there, so I took a peek. You know, just to find out what kind of stuff my little bro was into. So I figured you were gay. But I didn't think you were *like that*." Scott popped a corn fritter into his mouth. "So, like, do you want to"—he made a gesture with two fingers like a pair of scissors—"go all the way?"

George squeezed her legs together. "Maybe some-day," she said.

"Weird. But it kinda makes sense. No offense, but you don't make a very good boy."

"I know."

Mom returned to the table, and the conversation was dropped. All three of them stuffed their faces until they dragged their very full stomachs to the car, groan-ing all the way, much like Templeton the rat after his night of indulgence at the fair.

All three of them crashed in front of the television when they got home, and watched a sitcom about a family with twelve kids. The jokes mostly focused on the empty fridge and full bathroom. George wondered what it would be like to live with so many people. Maybe each kid got noticed less. With Mom eyeing her from her chair, George wondered whether maybe that wasn't such a bad thing.

Scott snuck glances her way too, but where Mom's eyes were filled with concern and confusion, Scott looked at George as if his sibling made sense to him for the first time. George had never been gladder to have an older brother.

chapter X

TRANSFORMATIONS

George wasn't sure when Jeff would be back at school, and every morning, she kept nervous eyes out for the first sign of his spiky hair. When she finally spotted it, Jeff was already headed in her direction with a sneer across his face. He walked at a steady pace, his eyes steeled in the distance beyond George. He didn't break his stride for an instant but spit at her feet as he passed. Every time he passed her that week, he spit. Real spit that landed on the pavement if they were outside, pretend spit on the linoleum floors if they were inside the school.

● ● ●

The morning of the play, the students of Room 205 chatted and laughed, leaving their bags on their desks and ignoring the assignment on the board. Only Ms. Udell's threat to cancel the play quieted the class, and even then, she struggled to wrangle her students through a morning of reading, journals, math, and vocabulary. Kelly and George exchanged knowing glances throughout.

After recess, Ms. Udell and Mr. Jackson brought their classes to the auditorium. Kindergarten through third-grade students filed noisily into the old wooden seats for the afternoon performance. Parents and relatives sat in the first few rows. Isaiah, the boy from Mr. Jackson's class who was playing Wilbur, frolicked heartily, getting into character.

The cast and stagehands gathered with Ms. Udell backstage. The rest of the class went to sit in the audience with Mr. Jackson. It was dark behind the thick red cloth that draped the stage, and the air smelled musty, but once the curtains were pulled, the light from the auditorium windows would fill the stage.

After the audience was seated, the overhead light flickered twice, signaling quiet. The curtain squeaked open and Jocelyn walked onstage. The girl from Mr. Jackson's class was playing Fern, and she carried a blanket in her arms, meant to represent the runt pig, Wilbur. For this scene, Wilbur didn't have anything to do or say but to be saved from Pa's ax, and Isaiah was too big for Jocelyn to hold him in her arms. The first narrator began to speak, and the play had begun.

When it was nearly time for Kelly's first lines, she stepped up the ladder, carefully holding her extra limbs in her hands. She gave her opening speech, which went perfectly. She even said *salutations* the right way. The audience was focused on her every move. She spotted her dad and winked at him. Then she climbed down to wait for her next scene.

"You were great!" George whispered when Kelly was back on the ground.

"You're gonna be even better!" Kelly whispered back.

George said nothing, but she pictured herself onstage, at the top of the ladder, sharing Charlotte's words with the audience.

The play was short, over before most of the younger students began to squirm in their seats. At the end, the actors took their bows and Ms. Udell thanked the members of the audience for their time.

Once the younger students had filed out, Ms. Udell spoke to the fourth graders and the family members in the audience. "Students who are performing this evening, please be back at five thirty. The play will begin at six sharp. Parents and family, I hope you'll stay for the PTA meeting that will follow." A few parents coughed in response. George knew that coughing was the adult equivalent of groaning.

Families congratulated the performers at the front of the stage. Kelly's dad had even brought a bouquet for her. He and other parents left with their children. Ms. Udell escorted the remainder of the class back to Room 205 for the final twenty minutes of the day, to write in their journals about *The Excitement of the Theatrical Experience*, which was what Ms. Udell wrote on the board in large letters.

George wrote a single sentence on her page: *It was exciting to help out with the play.* But what she really wanted to write was *I'm going to be Charlotte!!!!*

● ● ●

Mom arrived home right when it was time to head to school for the play. She didn't even bother to remove her shoes.

"Ready to go?" she asked.

Scott was at Randy's house for the evening,

supposedly working on a school project. George suspected that they were more likely watching gore flicks, but either way, she was glad Scott wasn't coming to the play. He had shown surprising tact until now, but if he said the wrong thing to Mom, he could really freak her out. George got up from the spot where she had been flopped on the couch for the last hour, barely noticing the talking dogs and superhero kids who flashed by on the television screen. She had bigger things on her mind. She put on her dress shoes, the only pair of black shoes she owned. When she was handing the spiderweb signs up to Kelly, her white sneakers hadn't mattered much, but if she was going to be Charlotte, she wanted to do it right.

As Mom pulled out of the driveway, George's stomach turned nervously. She counted telephone poles to relax.

"So how was the afternoon performance?" Mom asked.

"It was okay." George was used to counting while Mom talked. She held the tens on her fingers to keep track.

"That really sells it for me."

"Sorry, Mom. I was just thinking."

The ride to school wasn't long, so if George missed a pole, she might not have another chance to get up to one hundred. She supposed she didn't really need an imaginary electric fairy to go through with her and Kelly's plan, but it seemed safer that way.

"I'm excited to see you take a bow this evening, even as a stagehand. And Kelly will be great as Charlotte, I'm sure."

George didn't correct her. Mom would find out about the plan soon enough, and by then, it would be too late to stop it. George reached a hundred telephone poles with blocks to spare.

The tiny school parking lot was full, so Mom found a spot on the street a block away.

"Looks like it's going to be a big audience," Mom said.

"Guess so." George shrugged, trying to ignore the fear that coursed through her.

At the door of the auditorium, Mom kissed George on the cheek and searched for a seat. George could hear the students gathered backstage. The red curtain was heavy, and she fought her way through. The backstage lighting was dim, and George's eyes blinked to adjust. Most of the cast and crew were already assembled.

"There you are!" Kelly skipped over to George.

George grinned. They both wore all black. The only difference between their costumes was the vest of stuffed spider arms that Kelly wore. They shared secret smiles and giggles until it was nearly time for the show to begin. George shook with excitement.

"This is it, ladies and gents," said Mr. Jackson, gathering the cast and stagehands together. "Let's make

Mr. E. B. White proud one more time. Best performance and best behavior."

"Break a leg!" Ms. Udell said with a wink.

"Take your places and we'll get this show on the road!" Mr. Jackson twirled his index finger in the air.

Ms. Udell took the side steps off the stage and sat down in the first row of the audience. Mr. Jackson stayed backstage to oversee the performance.

The play began just as it had in the afternoon. The curtain rose on Fern Arable holding a blanket in her arms, cooing to a pretend piglet, and the audience applauded. The first narrator described the Arables' farm and told the audience about the baby pig who was moments from execution.

Backstage, Kelly took off the vest of spider arms and handed it to George, who checked to make sure that Mr. Jackson wasn't watching. Then she donned the vest. The fake arms were filled with cotton and didn't weigh much, but they were bulky. George had to bunch them up in her real arms, as she had seen Kelly do, to make sure she didn't trip over them. She combed her hair forward with her fingers, as she had done countless times in the mirror, and waited. The opening scenes of the play had never been so slow.

George was bouncing on the balls of her feet with nervous excitement by the time the barnyard animals began to greet Wilbur. Charlotte's first lines were only moments away. George climbed up the ladder to appear above the backdrop, in full view of the audience.

"Salutations!" George called out. Her voice was loud and clear, but with a soft lilt that showed Charlotte's kindness. She looked down to see Kelly holding the ladder steady with one hand as she took pictures of George with the other.

George heard a gasp onstage below her, and then another, but she kept going. She explained to the animals what *salutations* were. She smiled and waved to Wilbur and to the audience, as if she were saying hello to the world. The audience smiled back. A small kid even waved.

Ms. Udell sat in the middle of the front row, frowning, just as she had in the hallway after George's audition. George looked away. She looked for Mom, to see her reaction, but couldn't find her in the crowded auditorium.

The rest of the audience was watching her, waiting for Charlotte's next line, and George didn't disappoint. Every word sounded just as she had rehearsed it. She didn't make a single mistake. She felt like she was floating.

At the end of the scene, George climbed back down the ladder. Her body felt as light as air, and she wasn't completely sure her shoes were touching the ground. Kelly squeezed her from behind, grabbing the cotton arms along with George's waist.

"Wow, George, that was awesome!" she whispered. "Really."

"Thanks." George beamed a goofy, unfocused grin.

"You were totally like a girl." Kelly took George's hand, one of the real ones. "I mean, you totally *are* a girl." Kelly hugged her best friend tightly.

Jocelyn walked up to them, her fists in tight balls. "You can't just do that!" she whispered loudly.

"Why not?" Isaiah whispered back.

"Yeah." Chris crowded into the huddle backstage. "Why not? He was good. Better than Kelly, even. No offense, Kelly."

Kelly shrugged. "I wasn't that great."

"But it's disrupting to the other actors," said Emma.

Most of the narrators had joined the circle around George, as had a few of the barnyard animals, who were supposed to be clucking and mooing onstage. Rick remained by the curtain rope and said nothing.

"Hush." Mr. Jackson approached the group and herded it away from George and Kelly.

The side curtain moved, and Ms. Udell stepped backstage, her face in a scowl. She headed toward George, but Principal Maldonado appeared directly behind her and put her hand on Ms. Udell's shoulder. Then she whispered something into Ms. Udell's ear.

Ms. Udell looked at George, Kelly, and finally Principal Maldonado. She raised a finger and opened her mouth, but then stopped. She looked over at the play, still in progress, and the audience beyond. She gave a weak smile to Kelly, an even weaker smile to George, then stepped offstage.

Principal Maldonado gave George a subtle nod, more with her eyelids than her chin. Then she stepped offstage as well. By then, it was nearly time for Charlotte's next scene. George climbed carefully up the ladder and waited quietly for her cue.

The play passed by quickly, and yet it seemed to George as though she had been onstage since the beginning of time, as if she were born there and had only now found herself where she had always been. Wilbur performed his silly antics; Templeton raced around to gather sesquipedalian words; the geese clucked around and were generally a nuisance. It was like a real barnyard onstage.

And at the center of it all, Charlotte provided her friendship and wisdom. George reveled in every moment, sharing her voice with the audience and watching them watch her as they waited for her next words.

It wasn't long at all before George gave Charlotte's final speech. Charlotte was dying. It was the way of things, and she could do nothing but accept her fate. The sadness in George's voice came from deep inside; she knew her moment onstage was nearly over.

"Good-bye, Wilbur," she said as her last words floated into the audience and out of reach. Before she could bear to step down from the ladder, George looked up. Sad faces filled the audience, and younger kids wiped their eyes on their sleeves. Still, she didn't see Mom.

The moment George reached the ground, she cried too. She slumped against the backstage wall, hugging her knees, as she cried in sadness and joy. Charlotte was dead, but George was alive in a way she had never imagined. She watched the remainder of the show from the side of the stage, in a heady post-performance glow. Soon the audience began to clap.

Someone grabbed George's hand and brought her into the line of performers. Everyone bowed in unison. Then the human characters moved up for a second bow. The applause grew stronger as Chris, who had played Templeton, stepped forward. Isaiah hopped onto his hands and knees to oink like a pig once more, to laughter and even more applause.

George felt someone push her gently, and she let her feet guide her to the front of the stage. The auditorium was filled with hands clapping louder than ever. She blinked a few times, and then saw Ms. Udell motioning for her to bow.

George looked out on the crowd and did the only thing that made any sense. She curtsied. She wore no skirt to hold daintily, but she didn't need it. She was graceful, and she held on to the moment as tightly as she could, even after the curtains were pulled shut.

The class clapped and hooted and howled. A few kids patted George on the back. "Way to go," they said, and, "You were awesome!"

"Congratulations to you all!" Mr. Jackson cried as he stepped out from backstage. "You were fantastic! Including our surprise star!" Mr. Jackson smiled at George. "Now, there are a lot of excited families here, eager to congratulate you. I suggest you get out there!"

George worked her way through the split in the curtain and surveyed the audience. Kids weaved around, finding their parents and saying good night to their friends. Chris re-created some of his favorite moments.

Kelly bounced around, taking photos. Nearby, her father gave George a giant thumbs-up sign. In the back, Rick slipped out the auditorium door. He had come alone. George wondered whether he would say anything to Jeff.

George heard her name coming from kids talking to their parents, as well as the word *boy*. Adults' heads turned her way. Most looked at her with open faces of surprise. A few smiled and waved. Others crinkled their faces in disgust. George stepped offstage and out of view of staring eyes.

Mom made her way up the main aisle. Her stern face stood out in the crowd. George felt as if she were frozen in place.

"Well, that was unexpected," Mom said. "I didn't even know it was you at first. I thought it was supposed to be Kelly, but then I realized I was seeing my son onstage, and nearly everyone in the audience thought he was a girl."

George's lips quivered, but her voice was clear. "I did too."

"Did what?"

A bit of Charlotte's confidence still coursed through her. "I already told you. I'm a girl."

Mom's face turned to stone and her mouth grew small. "Let's not talk about this right now."

George noticed Principal Maldonado heading toward them, a soft smile on her face.

"Congratulations! You were wonderful!" she said to George, then turned to Mom. "Your kid was great tonight. You just might have a famous actor on your hands someday."

"Thank you." Mom smiled politely. "He certainly is special."

"Well, you can't control who your children are, but you can certainly support them, am I right?" Principal Maldonado's earrings sparkled in the auditorium light.

"Excuse us," said Mom, searching awkwardly in her purse for some imaginary item. "But we've got to get home to dinner."

"Well, make sure the star gets extra dessert tonight!" Principal Maldonado put her arm around George. She smelled of vanilla.

"I certainly will," said Mom.

"That was beautiful, George. Really beautiful." Ms. Maldonado put her lips close to George's ear and whispered, "My door is always open," before she slipped away.

Mom took George by the hand and walked brusquely through the lingering crowd. Once they were out in the hallway, the murmurs from the auditorium were quieter, and their footsteps echoed. Outside, it was dark enough that the streetlamps had turned on, but the sky still held a bit of light. Mom jiggled her keys in her palm. Neither she nor George said a word.

At home, they watched a dancing competition on television as they ate a dinner of spaghetti. Scott was still off at Randy's. George noticed that Mom kept looking over at George, but when George looked back, Mom had her eyes fixed on the television screen, even if it was showing commercials, which she usually hated.

Neither Mom nor George mentioned the play that evening, but once George was up in her room, she twirled around and around like a spider dancing on a web.

chapter XI

INVITATIONS

Kelly stood in a circle of girls in the school yard the next morning, telling an animated story, but she stopped when she spotted George. They pointed and called her over.

"And here's our hero!" said Kelly, smiling and holding her hands out as if she were a model presenting a new car on a game show.

"How did you know all the words?" Maddy asked.

"What was it like to play a girl onstage?" asked Ellie.

"I didn't even realize you were a boy at first," said Aliyah, a girl from Mr. Jackson's class who had been one of the barnyard animals.

"I heard you were really good," said Denise, who hadn't been there.

"I still don't think you should have done it," said Emma, who had been a narrator. "It could've messed everything up."

"Besides," said Jocelyn, "you're a boy. Why would you want to play a girl's part anyway?"

"I couldn't even imagine being a boy onstage, even if everyone knew I was really a girl. I just couldn't do it," said Maddy.

"Yeah, it would be too embarrassing," said Denise.

Comments came flashing at George faster than she could respond, which was a relief, because she didn't know what to say. Instead, she shrugged and smiled weakly. She wished she could be Charlotte now. Then she could answer all their buzzing with sage words of advice, instead of drowning in questions.

George heard dreadful laughter behind her. It was a

familiar snicker that swelled into a snorting guffaw—
Jeff's laugh. Before she could prepare, Jeff was in front
of her, Rick at his side. Jeff pushed George's shoulders
with the base of his hands. He didn't push hard, but
George hadn't been ready, and she stumbled back. The
crowd of girls dispersed, leaving Jeff and Rick facing
George and Kelly.

Jeff snickered again. "I heard you were in our class
play, *Charlotte*."

"He was, and he was great!" said Kelly.

"Oh, shut up. I'm talking to George here. He's more
of a girl than you'll ever be."

"Leave her alone!" George yelled.

"Or else what?" asked Jeff.

"Just leave her alone." George stared at the ground.

"C'mon, Jeff. Let's go." Rick tugged at Jeff's elbow.
"You promised if I told you what happened that you
wouldn't mess with him."

"Whatever," said Jeff, flicking his finger on George's forehead. "This freak pukes. I like this shirt, and my mom still can't get his stink out of the last one."

Jeff cracked up and walked off with Rick.

"Forget them," said Kelly. "I've got a surprise. My uncle Bill's taking us to the zoo on Sunday!"

George crinkled her nose. Zoo air smelled like animal poop. Besides, she and Kelly had decided last year that the Smithfield petting zoo was for babies. They had more ducks than anything else, and their most exotic showing was a crusty old pony that had recently celebrated its fortieth birthday.

"Not the Smithfield Snoozefest, you dope." Kelly rolled her eyes. "He's gonna drive us down to the Bronx Zoo. They have over six hundred species. Tigers and gorillas and giraffes, not goats and sheep. They've even got panda bears! You're free on Sunday, right?"

"I guess," George said.

"Because I was thinking." Kelly lowered her voice. "The Bronx Zoo is super-far away, and we won't see anyone there we know. You've never met my uncle, have you?"

George shook her head.

Kelly grinned. "Don't you get it? We can go as *best girl friends*. We can dress up and everything!"

George's mouth hung open. George already knew Kelly was her best friend, but they had never been girls together before. George had never been a girl with anyone, if you didn't count being Charlotte.

"Did you hear me?"

"Like a skirt?" The hair on George's neck tingled just saying the word *skirt*.

"Sure. When *girls* dress up, they wear skirts. I have a lot to teach you about being a girl, Geor—Oh." Kelly stopped. "My uncle's going to figure out something's up the moment I call you George, isn't he?"

George thought about her private name. She had never said it out loud before, not even to her friends in the magazines. "You could always call me Melissa," she said now.

"Melissa," said Kelly, her eyes wide. "I like it. That's a great name for a girl." She said it again, drawing out each sound. "Me-lis-sa. That's perfect!"

George buried her chin in her shoulder and felt her cheeks grow warm.

"Are you okay?" Kelly asked.

"Yeah," said George. "It just sounds really good to hear."

"I can say it again. Melissa. Melissa Melissa Melissa!" Kelly began to twirl around George, stretching her arms out wide with each *Melissa*.

George clapped her hand over Kelly's mouth.

"Are you crazy? Jeff is right over there!" George jerked her head to the side.

"So? I've got a friend named Melissa. He doesn't know who I'm talking about. It's none of his business anyway."

Kelly danced around George, singing the name *Melissa* until George giggled and turned beet red. She had never heard her girl name out loud before, and now Kelly had made it into a song.

The morning bell rang and the mass of students in the school yard formed into a series of lines. As George walked up the stairs to Room 205, she listened to Kelly's tune still echoing in her mind.

Melissa Melissa Melissa . . .

● ● ●

Mom was sitting on the couch when George got home, her laptop in front of her and a can of orange-flavored seltzer on the side table. A soap opera ran on the television with the sound turned low.

"Come over here, Gee." Mom patted the space on the couch next to her, closed the computer, and turned off the television. She took a few deep breaths before speaking.

"You were great in the play yesterday. I know I acted surprised at first, but I'm really proud of you for being yourself. What did the kids at school say?"

George shrugged. "Not much. Jeff was a jerk."

"What's new? You're one tough cookie. But the world isn't always good to people who are different. I just don't want you to make your road any harder than it has to be."

"Trying to be a boy is really hard."

Mom blinked a few times, and when she opened her eyes again, a teardrop fell down her cheek.

"I'm sorry, Gee. I'm so sorry." She pulled George toward her and hugged her tight. "You really do feel like a girl, don't you?"

"Yeah, I do. Remember that time I was little, when you found me wearing your skirt as a dress?"

"Yes."

"And remember how I wanted to be a ballerina and it drove Scott crazy because he said I couldn't because I was a boy?"

"I remember the temper tantrum you threw when I didn't get you a tutu."

"Are you upset with me?"

"Oh, baby, no." Mom stroked George's hair and sighed deeply. "But I do think you need someone to talk to. I probably could use someone too. Someone who knows about these things."

George knew that seeing a therapist was the first step secret girls like her took when they wanted everyone to see who they were. "And then maybe I could grow my hair out and be a girl?"

"One step at a time." Mom wiped away another tear that had drifted down to her cheek. She cleared her throat. "Now how's about that homework?"

George pulled out her vocabulary assignment and

began to work at the table while Mom went to the kitchen to start making dinner. Mom poured a box of corn bread mix into a bowl along with eggs and milk. George noticed that she mixed with quiet efficiency, holding her whisking arm tight to her body. She didn't hum or dance the way she often did when she cooked.

The house was quiet until Scott arrived home with the clatter of his bike hitting the pavement. He dashed through the house and up to the bathroom.

"Ahhhhhh," he said when he sauntered back down the stairs. "No wonder they call it relieving yourself. That was a good one!"

"Scott, go put your bike in the shed. And, Gee, set the table. It's almost dinnertime."

Mom portioned grilled chicken wings with barbecue sauce, corn bread, and steamed broccoli onto three plates, and set them out on the table. George filled three glasses with iced tea and brought out forks, knives, and napkins.

Over dinner, Scott complained about the unfairness of his latest social studies test, and told the story of Mike the Headless Chicken, a real chicken that had lived without a head for eighteen months in the 1940s. When Scott acted out the part of Mike, using the chicken wings on his plate, George laughed so hard she almost choked. Even Mom chuckled.

And that night, when George went to her bedroom, she found her denim bag on her bed, with all of her magazines still inside.

chapter XII

MELISSA GOES TO THE ZOO

George awoke before the sun and couldn't fall back asleep. She'd never been this excited for the zoo before, not even when she was little. When the dark cloudy sky revealed its first shades of purple, George slipped out of bed and settled down on the couch with some cereal and the remote control, but nothing on television caught her interest. It was too early for anything good to be on. She tried playing *Mario Kart* but kept losing focus and falling into deep lava pits.

The sky had begun to lighten, but there were still nearly two hours before she was supposed to leave for

Kelly's house. She went out to the backyard, where her sneakers squeaked on the dew-soaked spring grass.

In the far corner of the yard was an old oak tree, and tied to one of the lowest branches of the tree was an old-fashioned swing. George's dad had hung it after he and Mom separated, but before he left town. A plank of wood hung from two thick lengths of rope, with a stretch of bare dirt below, where years of feet had worn away the grass. The seat had once been bright red, but what was now left of the paint was dull and chipped, revealing the gray wood beneath. Once, Scott and George had fought for turns on the swing. Sometimes they even swung on it together. Scott hadn't used the swing in a long time, though, and even George hadn't been on it since last year.

George brushed the seat with the elbow of her jacket and sat down. She took small steps backward until she stood on tiptoe, the seat pressed against her behind.

Then she lifted her toes, leaned back in the seat, and glided into the morning air. She coasted for a bit and then began to pump her legs, rising higher and higher. Soon, she was able to see into the neighbor's yard with each lift into the sky.

The light in the east was still orange from the sunrise. The sun itself had lifted into the sky, and its rays were warm on George's face each time she emerged from the shade of the old oak tree. She swung for a long time, enjoying the rhythm and the breeze.

She wondered what kind of skirt she would wear, and whether she and Kelly would match. And she wondered what Kelly's uncle Bill would be like. If he was as clueless as Scott, he would never notice that George wasn't a regular girl. If he *did* notice, George wasn't sure whether he would be nice. Kelly said he was nice, but Kelly had been wrong before. He might laugh at George. He might even leave her at the zoo. Still, there was no way she was going to pass up this chance to be a girl with Kelly.

When George came inside, Mom was at the stove with a spatula, tending to a frying pan. She wore an apron that said MIND THE CHEF in large letters. The air smelled sweet, and George's stomach growled.

"You want pancakes?" Mom asked.

"Yes, please. With cinnamon."

George toyed with telling Mom about the plan, but she remembered Mom's words: *one step at a time.* She would tell Mom about her adventure when Mom was ready. Instead, they talked about the animals George would see, as if it were any other trip to the zoo.

After breakfast, George pulled out her bike and put on her helmet. She rode past the library and up the hill to the corner store where Mom sometimes sent her to pick up milk or a loaf of bread. She rode past the big purple house with a cactus garden for a front yard, and past the building where her old babysitter used to live. She rode alongside the cemetery twice—up the slow and steady incline, around the back, and *swoosh*, down the trail on the far side, with its three bumps down.

When she couldn't bear waiting any longer, she headed toward Kelly's house. George pedaled as slowly as she could manage to stay upright, riding up and down side streets, but she still arrived fifteen minutes early. She waited around outside until she thought her head would pop.

When she finally knocked, the door opened instantly. Kelly pulled George into the main room of the basement apartment. She wore green pajamas and her hair was tied back in a puff of curls. "Finally, you're here! We can get dressed!"

"What if your dad wakes up and sees us?" whispered George, looking over at Kelly's father asleep on the daybed.

"Are you kidding me? He had a gig at the Masons' Lodge last night. He won't move until noon." Kelly gestured her thumb at her snoring father. "If he does see anything, he'll think it's a dream."

Kelly led George into her room and shut the door behind her. The closet and most of her dresser drawers were open, displaying an array of girls' clothing, and Kelly had laid out an assortment of makeup on her desk. The air smelled of perfume, several bottles of which were lined in a neat row next to the makeup.

"Welcome to Kelly's Salon. Whaddaya think?"

George's heart thumped in her chest. It was as if all of the pages of all of her magazines had come to life in Kelly's bedroom.

"It's . . . wonderful."

"What do you want to try on first?"

"What *can* I try on?"

"Anything you want!"

George looked over the skirts that hung in Kelly's

closet. She had no idea how to choose. "What do you think would look good on me?"

"I have the perfect thing." Kelly sounded like a clerk at a high-end clothing boutique. She dashed to the closet and pulled out a flared skirt of purple swirls and rummaged through a drawer for a hot-pink tank top. She laid the clothing in George's hands. The top was soft, softer than any boys' shirt she had ever worn. And she had never held a skirt in her hands like this before. Together, they felt magical.

"I didn't even know you had any skirts," said George.

"I don't wear them to school. Boys are dirty and try to look up them."

"*I'd* never try to look up your skirt."

"Of course not. You're not a boy."

"Oh, right." George laughed. Even she was sometimes fooled by her body. Kelly laughed too, and no one passing by the basement apartment window would have ever suspected that there weren't two girls in the room below, bonding over clothes, boys, and whatever else it was girls gossiped about.

"So," Kelly said, "don't you want to try them on?"

George nodded slowly. "Could you turn around?"

"Of course!" Kelly turned back to the closet and held shirts and skirts against each other, looking for the perfect match.

George eyed the tank top Kelly had given her. It looked a bit like an undershirt, but with thinner shoulder straps. She took off her T-shirt and slipped the girls' top over her head. The air felt cool on her exposed shoulders. Next, she took off her sweatpants and stepped into the skirt. She pulled it up to her waist and let the fabric settle into place.

She looked in the mirror and gasped. Melissa gasped back at her. For a long time, she stood there, just blinking. George smiled, and Melissa smiled too.

When her eyes started to sting, she twirled in a circle, and the skirt ballooned out below. Stopping with her legs crossed, she felt like a model.

Kelly squealed when she turned around. "Oh, that looks so cute on you . . . Melissa."

Melissa's heart fluttered, hearing her name.

"Can I take a picture?" Kelly snapped her camera before Melissa could answer.

"Now try these on." She handed Melissa a yellow skirt with shimmering fringe at the bottom and a black T-shirt with a yellow heart in the center.

Melissa fingered the fringe of the skirt. She didn't want to take off the clothes she was already wearing, but the fringe looked so lovely, and it would brush against her knees as she moved.

Kelly turned back to the closet, and Melissa changed shirts. She stepped into the yellow skirt and brought it up to her waist. Again, she gazed in the mirror, amazed to find herself there. She could have stared for a long time, but Kelly wanted to know what Melissa thought of her ensemble.

"Don't I look elegant? New York City's really elegant, you know." Kelly wore a long black skirt, a black top, and black silk gloves.

Melissa frowned. "You look like you're going to a zoo funeral."

Kelly laughed. "Yeah, you're right," she said, pulling the gloves back off by their fingers.

Melissa tried on half a dozen outfits in a whirlwind. Before she could change out of one, Kelly had another ready, and took half a dozen pictures of Melissa in each. Melissa didn't know whether to laugh or cry as she modeled the girls' clothing, with Kelly oohing and aahing all the way. She held the fabrics delicately, as if they would break, and rubbed them softly between her thumb and forefinger.

For all the different outfits she tried on, though, Melissa couldn't keep her mind off the first.

"You said it was perfect," she said to Kelly. "And you were right!"

Kelly gave up and Melissa delightedly put the pink tank top and purple skirt back on. She twirled in the center of the room, giddy on freedom. Kelly settled on a pink T-shirt that said ANGEL in glittery yellow letters, which she paired with the yellow fringed skirt.

Kelly sat Melissa down in a chair in front of the mirror and began to brush Melissa's hair. She tried brushing it first to one side, and then the other, but decided finally to brush it forward so that the tips of it fell just above Melissa's eyebrows.

"What if your uncle figures out I'm not *really* a girl?" Melissa asked.

"Look at you. Why would he think you're anything else?"

Kelly was right. Melissa's frame was thin, and she was too young to be expected to have curves. She was wearing girls' clothes and a girl's hairdo, even if it was short. She really did look like a girl.

Kelly gestured at her desk. "I've got all this makeup my aunt gave me for my birthday, but I don't really know how to put it on."

"I've never had any," said Melissa, "but I've read all about it."

Kelly handed her a small container of lip gloss. Melissa dipped her finger into the slippery, shiny substance and traced her lips. When she looked in the mirror, her lips sparkled.

Melissa and Kelly tried out every shade of gloss and blush in the kit. Melissa showed Kelly how to apply the blush high on the cheekbone and then blend downward, and how to choose colors to complement her light-brown skin. They amassed a great pile of tissues as they wiped off one color and replaced it with another. They smiled for the mirror and each other. Kelly took photo after photo.

"Oh, no!" Melissa cried suddenly. Her glee was replaced with dread as she looked down at her sock-covered feet. She pointed over to her ratty sneakers.

"You think I don't have that covered?" Kelly pulled a bucket of shoes from under her bed.

"You have so many shoes. Who knew you were such a girly girl?"

"Who knew *you* were?" Kelly grinned. She rummaged through the pile and handed Melissa a simple pair of white sandals. They were a little small on Melissa's feet, but since they were sandals, it didn't matter too much. Kelly found a pair of yellow canvas sneakers to match her own skirt.

They were ready, but Uncle Bill hadn't arrived yet, so Kelly turned cartwheels across the carpet. Half the time, her skirt would flip right over her belly, leaving her pink underwear showing. She would scamper down and smooth out her skirt, but that didn't stop her from trying again. Melissa was looking at her reflection from every angle she could. She faced away from the big mirror and held a hand mirror so she could see her back.

"Kelly?" Melissa stopped her friend while she was upright. "There's just one more thing."

"Melissa, stop worrying. You look perfect."

"It's just . . . I'm wearing boys' underpants." Melissa felt the wide band of elastic around her waist that held up her white boys' briefs. No one would be able to see them, but she would know all day that they were there.

"Ew! Yuck! Pull them off!" Kelly was already at her dresser drawer. She handed Melissa a pair of light-pink underwear covered in tiny red hearts. They were small and light. "You can have them. Don't worry. They're clean."

"Are you sure?" Melissa asked.

"Of course. I have too many pairs anyway."

Melissa turned around and began to take off the purple skirt.

"You don't have to take it off. You can change under it. Skirts are awesome like that."

"Oh, right."

Melissa took off her own underwear, stepped into Kelly's, and pulled it up under her skirt. Other than the coolness of the fabric on her skin, she could barely tell she was wearing anything at all.

Kelly jumped up when she heard a knock on the front door. "Let's go!"

Kelly let her uncle into the small apartment. Bill Arden could have been his brother's twin, right down to the friendly twinkle in his deep-brown eyes. He was a painter; bright streaks of blue and red stained his sneakers.

"Well, you girls are dressed mighty fancy for the zoo," Uncle Bill remarked.

"It's not often a handsome man invites us out to New Yawwk City." Kelly pronounced the name of the metropolis as though she had been raised deep in the country.

"At least you're wearing practical shoes, which is more than I can say for most of the women I take out on the town. Although it's not often that I'm graced with the company of two fine young women at once. Kelly, who's your lovely friend?"

"This is Melissa. She's a bit shyer than I am."

Melissa was afraid to move, nervous that a single step could break the magic.

"Pleased to meet you, Melissa." Uncle Bill's hand was large and his handshake was firm, but not tight. "And as for you, my dear niece," he continued, hugging Kelly to his side, "I do believe a rampaging rhinoceros would be shyer than you are."

"I doubt that," said Kelly. "But there's only one way to find out. To the zoo!" Kelly grabbed two of her jackets, handed one to Melissa, and skipped down the cracked pavement to Uncle Bill's car.

The ride down to the zoo took nearly two hours, with Uncle Bill singing loudly and off-key to disco songs on the radio. Kelly sang along when she knew the words. Melissa sat beside her in the backseat, admiring the swirls in her skirt. She fingered its hem, just a little heavier than the rest of the fine cloth. She brushed her palms down the tank top she wore, and combed her fingers through her hair. She reached out her hand and Kelly squeezed it in hers.

If Melissa held her body just right, she could see herself in the car's rearview mirror. It was hard to keep from giggling with delight. She looked out the window and counted a hundred telephone poles. Twice. Both times, she wished she could be like this forever.

Finally, Melissa saw a big green sign for the Bronx Zoo with a thick arrow pointing to the right. Uncle Bill drove off the highway, and soon they were paying a fee to enter a massive parking lot. Uncle Bill drove down a long line of cars and pulled into a spot at the end.

The air smelled mostly like grass and hay, with a hint of animal poop. Melissa knew the smell would grow stronger, but she didn't care. She would be walking around all day dressed as a girl. Children and adults and even the animals would see her, and no one but she and Kelly would know a thing.

Around them, adults wrestled with babies and strollers, while older children stood around waiting. Kelly, Melissa, and Uncle Bill walked toward the entrance booth. There was a short line, but it moved quickly, and soon they were inside.

Melissa and Kelly laughed at the playing monkeys, shuddered past the slithering snakes, cooed at the baby grizzly bears, and stared at the tigers' teeth. Melissa surprised herself when she noticed her reflection in the glass in front of a display of exotic, glowing jellyfish. She was looking at a girl.

Melissa stopped at the tarantula exhibit. The furry crawlers were a much larger species of spider than Charlotte had been. Still, Melissa thanked each one quietly. She searched for webs, but didn't see any.

When they stepped out of the World of Insects, Kelly said she needed to use the bathroom. Melissa tensed. There was no way she could make it back home without going as well. She looked down at her skirt. She couldn't go into the boys' bathroom looking like this.

"Melissa and I will be right back," Kelly announced, grabbing her best friend by the hand before she could protest, dragging her right to a door with a sign with the word LADIES and a stick figure wearing a triangle skirt. Kelly pushed open the heavy metal bathroom door as if it were nothing and pulled Melissa in.

The air was cool, wet, and smelled of musk. The tiles were gray and green, not pink as Melissa had imagined. Most noticeably, there were no urinals, only a row of stalls on the left and a row of sinks, mirrors, and dispensers oozing pink soap on the right.

"You okay?" asked Kelly.

Melissa nodded but didn't say anything. She was

standing in the girls' room. Not even the eloquent Charlotte had a word for how she felt in that moment.

Melissa locked herself in a stall, delighted for the privacy. She lifted her skirt to see her underwear, covered in tiny red hearts. She pulled it down, sat, and peed, just like a girl. She didn't even tell Kelly afterward. That part of this magnificent day was her personal secret.

By early afternoon, Kelly, Melissa, and Bill were tired and hungry. Kelly found a meal station on the map just past Tiger Mountain. They smelled the food before they spotted a cluster of picnic benches set up around a bird-filled pond. Orange umbrellas advertising fruit smoothies shaded dozens of families. Some folks ate burgers and hot dogs and fries, while others munched on sandwiches and snacks pulled out of coolers from home. Strollers littered the walkways, with young children weaving between them and screaming with glee.

Uncle Bill took orders for lunch and stood in line while Kelly and Melissa waited for a table.

"So," Kelly said, "I call today a success. I'm already thinking about what to wear next time."

"You mean you'd do this again?"

"*Melissa.*" Kelly rolled her eyes. "I'm surrounded by boys in my life. My father. My uncle. Seriously, until a few weeks ago, I thought you were a boy. It's nice to have some girl time."

"Well, you two look happy!" said Uncle Bill, setting down a tray laden with sodas, hot dogs, a container of ketchup, and a giant cup of fries.

"We are," said Kelly.

A wave of warmth filled Melissa from deep in her belly and out to her fingers and toes. She put her arm around Kelly. Kelly held her camera at arm's length and took a picture of the two girls' grinning faces.

● ● ●

Kelly took dozens more photos of Melissa that afternoon. And Kelly didn't ask Melissa to pose once. She didn't have to. Melissa already looked perfect in every one.

By the time they loaded into the car, Kelly, Uncle Bill, and Melissa were all exhausted, even though the sun was only just setting. Uncle Bill stopped off for coffee to stay awake and Kelly passed out as soon as they hit the highway. But Melissa didn't nod off for a moment. She couldn't. She was too busy remembering the best week of her life.

So far.

ACKNOWLEDGMENTS

I am inexpressibly indebted to so many people who have helped my baby grow over the last twelve years from "There should be a book about a trans kid!" to the story you hold in your hands. And yet, let me try.

Deepest and sincerest gratitude to Jean Marie Stine, without whom this book would still be a pile of chapters on a long-defunct hard drive. Infinite thanks to my aerobics instructor of an agent, Jennifer Laughran: "You're doing great! Just one more revision!" And with great appreciation for my editor, David Levithan, whose relentless enthusiasm for George is downright inspiring. Thanks to Ellen Duda for a cover that brought me tears of joy and to the copy editors who perfected every last dot and dash.

Powerful fondness and dearness for Beth Kelly, my oldest writing buddy, and Blake C. Aarens, my newest writing buddy. And so much love and thankfulness for the endless friends and family who read this story in its many stages: my parents, Cindy and Steve Gino, and my sister, Robin Gino Gridgeman. My dear partner in life, James McCormack. And Amy Benson, Lilia Schwartz, Matilda St. John, and Amithyst Fist.

And to the friends and family whose love and support allowed me to write and finish this book. Nana and Papa Gino, Aunt Sue, Uncle Paul, Nana and Rick Scott, Aunt Jerilynn, Wes, Anna, Kadyn, and Brinley. And Sondra Solovay, Joe Libin, Frankie Hill, Alicia Stephen, NOLOSE and all the radical fats, and so many more people—I would need another book to thank you all. I love you more than I know how to tell you.

ABOUT THE AUTHOR

Alex Gino loves glitter, ice cream, gardening, awe-ful puns, and stories that reflect the diversity and complexity of being alive. *George* is their first novel. For more about Alex, please visit www.alexgino.com.